Non-fiction Books By The Same Author

PEOPLE WHO MAKE THINGS:
How American Craftsmen Live and Work

AMISH PEOPLE:
Plain Living In A Complex World

ESKIMOS:
Growing Up In A Changing Culture

(MARGARET K. MC ELDERRY BOOKS)

C.C.
Poindexter

C.C.
Poindexter

CAROLYN MEYER

A MARGARET K. McELDERRY BOOK

Atheneum   1979   *New York*

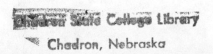

Library of Congress Cataloging in Publication Data
Meyer, Carolyn.
C. C. Poindexter.
"A Margaret K. McElderry book."
SUMMARY: The complicated lives of C. C.'s
family and friends fall into new patterns
the summer she is fifteen.
I. Title.
PZ7.M5685Cac   [Fic]   78-6102
ISBN 0-689-50119-6

Published simultaneously in Canada by
McClelland & Stewart, Ltd.
Printed and bound by
Fairfield Graphics,
Fairfield, Pennsylvania
Designed by Marjorie Zaum

First Printing August 1978
Second Printing February 1979

C.C.
Poindexter

Chapter One

 The van was painted purplish-red, the color of bad skin, and it stalled whenever it stopped moving. While we waited for the red light to change, my aunt Charlotte raced the engine, but it died anyway, right in front of the library where all the kids my age huddle along the brick wall waiting for something to happen. The stalling of the van was probably the most interesting event of the evening.

Both sides of the van were decorated with murals that showed women driving tractors, leading wagon trains, climbing into airplane cockpits, descending in diving bells, planting flags on top of snow-capped mountains. No matter what else they were doing, all the women stared straight out from the sides of the van, directly into the eyes of whoever was looking. The kids stared back at them.

On the back of the van above the rear engine where the starter still whined without catching, WOMAN POWER was painted in white letters designed to be visible at a distance. A fist was clenched with the female symbol on the door next to my aunt, and on my side, just beneath the window facing the library crowd, it said SISTERS UNITE. The sign across the front was lettered backward so that the driver of the car ahead could read it frontward in his or her rearview mirror: ЯƎⱭИU MOЯꟻ ꟼU.

A kid in a knitted hockey cap and patched jeans needing more patches hauled himself off the brick wall and ambled toward us. He kept his hands balled in the pockets over his stomach because it was March and still very cold. While my aunt pumped the accelerator and the ignition whirred and chuckled, the light turned green and traffic began to edge by us. The kid walked slowly all around the van. His teeth were bare to show he thought something was funny, and he made whinnying noises through his nose. He could not read backward, and he called over a buddy with a scrabbly little beard to decipher ЯƎⱭИU MOЯꟻ ꟼU. I recognized the buddy from one of my study halls. They howled, guffawed, slapped each other on the backs of their fake-leather jackets. Neither of them could see the huge women's liberation symbol painted on the roof for the benefit of people in low-flying planes and tall buildings.

The one who could read backward stuck his face up against the window on the driver's side. "Hey, lady," he drawled, "you need a *man* to show you how to handle that big ol' truck?"

I scrooched down in my seat and feigned invisibility. My aunt ignored him and glared at me. "C.C. Poindexter, sit up tall!" she commanded. "Be proud!" Then the engine caught, the van lurched, the boys jumped clear, and we shot forward. I could hear them roaring with laughter.

The van had been painted by my Aunt Charlotte,

who had also hung tie-dyed curtains at its windows so she could use it as a camper when she was attending women's meetings and craft fairs. Charlotte is the sister of my father, who no longer lives with us, but I am not supposed to call her *Aunt* Charlotte because she does not believe in titles of any kind, including *Mother*. She is a very interesting and persuasive person, and she had invited me to go to her women's rap group that night. She said it would give me a chance to ventilate my feelings against the male oppressors, such as the boys in front of the library.

My mother, who drives a station wagon with metal paneling painted to look like wood and who refuses to display a bumper sticker even for worthy causes like protecting the environment, does not approve of the rap group, or of the liberation movement, or of being called Margaret by my sister and me.

"They're a bunch of disappointed man-haters," my mother said when I told her about being invited to the group. But she didn't forbid me to go, and I told Charlotte yes, partly because Charlotte is my favorite adult, not counting parents (and sometimes counting them), and partly because I was curious.

"You know, C.C.," my aunt said, easing the van through an orange light at the next corner, "you're going to have to get used to confrontations like that one. That's a problem we women have to overcome. We tend to *shrink*, physically and emotionally, in the face of masculine aggression."

"I could use a little of that physical shrinkage," I said. Shrinkage is definitely not one of my problems. I hit an even six feet around the time of my fourteenth birthday, and a year later I had added another inch. Not yet sixteen and still growing. That's about ten inches more than I knew what to do with. I just do not have the personality for a tall person. Now Charlotte, who is only five feet seven, would love to be about six-three. She would probably *enjoy* being called Gulliver. I do not. I have a personality suitable for somebody very short. A dwarf, maybe; a Lilliputian.

"Nonsense!" Charlotte said firmly, nursing the engine at a red light she couldn't avoid. "Tall is beautiful!"

That's the kind of thing you can say if you aren't. If you are, tall is clumsy, hard to fit, and sometimes very amusing to other people. "How's the weather up there?" is typical of the kind of humor you attract. Charlotte would have a comeback for that. "Grow up and find out for yourself," was the cleverest retort I could manage, and pretty feeble at that.

"It may be beautiful," I agreed, "but Mom is afraid I won't be able to have what she calls a 'normal social life.' "

"A normal social life!" Charlotte shouted, getting excited. "And what, may I ask, is your mother's idea of a normal social life?"

"It means having dates when you're sixteen and later on getting a husband," I explained. I sort of agreed with my mother. For a girl, being too tall is even worse than being too intelligent. If you're really bright, like my best friend Laura, you can hide it if you want to, even though Laura never bothers. But you can't hide being tall, no matter how much you want to or how clever you are.

"Far be it from me to challenge your mother's idea of what a normal social life ought to be," Charlotte said, gunning up the ramp onto the thruway. "Your mother is very intelligent and talented, but she hasn't found herself or her direction. She's still quite obviously grieving over the divorce. Personally, I think she shows all the signs of becoming embittered. She's trying to hang onto a lifestyle that is no longer viable. And I have a hunch that she is really not the person to be deciding for you or for anyone else what a 'normal social life' should be."

"Umm," I replied, not exactly leaping to my mother's defense. Charlotte was also divorced, and she was launching into one of her favorite subjects.

"One of these days," Charlotte continued, "I hope your mother will enjoy freedom and total independence as much as I do. Self-reliance should be every woman's goal."

My mother and my aunt were natural enemies, and I was always changing sides, as I listened to one and then the other. They never squared off against each other anywhere but in my head. For instance, Mom always puts her children first, and before that her husband, when she had one. She sews all her own clothes and things for my sister Allison and me and taught us both how to do it, although I never had the patience for sewing. Once she made slipcovers for the living room sofa and three chairs and draperies to match. The house is always perfectly clean and neat, except for my room and any other room in which I have recently spent more than fifteen minutes.

My mother was a language major in college, and she planned to live in Italy after she graduated. She spoke Italian fluently, and when she met my father she impressed him because she could recite Dante. Then they got married and had me and then Allison, and my mother joined the American Association of University Women, which Charlotte defined as a bunch of women with good educations who don't know what to do with them. My father did not forget her dream, though, and one Christmas he bought her a pasta-maker. We had homemade lasagne and ravioli and every kind of spaghetti and macaroni you could think of. But when my father left she stopped all that and we settled down to practical budget meals, like meatloaf with lots of oatmeal as an extender. "There's no point in fancy cooking without a man around to eat it," she said. I don't think she remembered any Dante at all.

Charlotte is an artist-craftsperson, and she teaches art in our high school. She works hard at never asking anybody for help. She took an adult education course in auto mechanics so she could repair the van, which was always breaking down, and she had also studied plumbing and electricity. She could change the washers in the faucet when it leaked, and she replaced the ballcock valve in the toilet. Nothing was wrong with the wiring in her house, but she never gave up hope that something would short out on her and she could come to her own rescue.

It was my mother's opinion that Charlotte wasn't kidding anybody except possibly herself. "Every woman is better off with a man, and your aunt is no exception," she said. "And what about her two sons? Maybe Charlotte can tune an engine, but she couldn't handle her own children. Otherwise they would not have left," she said flatly, which means you can't disagree.

My cousin Jebby had gone to live with his father in Oregon two years ago. Charlotte said that was just fine with her, because fathers have as much responsibility for bringing up children as mothers do, and since Uncle Ted earns a lot more money than she does, why shouldn't he? Michael took off and joined a commune in Virginia. "I raised my children to be independent," she said, "and if that's how he wants to live his life, it's not up to me to interfere." She had even given her written consent, since he was under age and Wisdom Peak wouldn't accept him without her signature.

"Ha," my mother snorted. "Charlotte never paid enough attention to either one of those boys, or to Ted either, for that matter. No wonder they all left." It was clear to my mother why Uncle Ted left Charlotte, but I don't think it was so clear to my mother why my father left *her*. Not from neglect, that's for sure. But why was it? I don't know either. You can live your whole life with people and never know some of the most important things about them.

While Michael was still at home with Charlotte, he used to come over to our place a lot. My mother fed him homemade cookies and hot chocolate and hauled out her sewing machine to fix his clothes and then put them through the washer. "I don't believe in doing things for a sixteen-year-old kid that he can jolly well do for himself," Charlotte said.

"That boy needs a *mother*," Mom always said after he went home again with his stomach filled and his clothes fixed. Then one day she suggested I sew up his ripped jeans. "Michael is a boy," she explained, "and you certainly can't expect him to run a sewing machine." I did it, but I was relieved when I heard he had gone to live in Virginia.

"If you spend so much time with Charlotte, you'll end up like her, I'm afraid," my mother warned me as I was about to race out to meet my aunt that evening before the engine quit. "She's obviously not a very happy person."

"If you're not careful, C.C.," Charlotte said now,

shifting into fourth, "you'll end up just like your mother. A nice person, but look at the mess she's in!"

I tried to change the subject. "What do you hear from Michael?"

"Hey, I almost forgot to tell you! He wants me to come down and spend a few days at Wisdom Peak and see what it's like."

"That sounds really good. Are you going?"

"I wouldn't miss it. He says before I come there I have to read a couple of books about their particular philosophical concept. It's based on behaviorism—you know, you get rewards when you do the right thing. It all sounds very complicated to me: labor credit systems and planning boards and so on. Visitors there have to work if they stay for more than twenty-four hours. He says I'll have to earn my keep."

"I wish I could go too," I said, not knowing I wanted to until I said it and then wanting to very much.

"Well, why not?"

That's what I really like about my aunt. She's game for anything. But I could think of at least one good reason why not: my mother. She had become very negative, to say the least, about everything I wanted to do. Not only did she say no most of the time, but she also said, "Now I don't want any further discussion," or, "The subject is closed," which meant you couldn't even ask for a reasonable explanation.

The home of Moozy von Schmidt where the rappers were meeting that evening was three towns up the thruway. After passing blocks of small apartment buildings with balconies and wrought-iron light fixtures and names like "The Regency," Charlotte turned in at a gate with signs in stylish block letters on both white pillars: "Les Artistes." Beyond the gate was a complex of buildings that looked as though a stack of gigantic kindergarten blocks had been abandoned. They lay at odd angles among neat rows of spindly trees. While Charlotte circled slowly, hunting for a parking spot, I read the names on each of the blocks: Van Gogh. Picasso. Rembrandt. "That topless pyramid over there is where Moozy lives. The Matisse. Our group is petitioning to have the name changed from Matisse to Cassatt."

"Cassatt? Was he a painter?"

The engine died on cue. "*Mary* Cassatt," Charlotte explained patiently, "happens to have been one of the greatest Impressionist painters of all time. American, too."

"Oh."

"Don't blame yourself. It's our male-dominated educational system." She got the engine going again and wedged the van neatly into a narrow slot. "Funny thing is, Moozy is leading the Cassatt battle, but we can't get her to do a thing about her own name. She says she doesn't want to resume her maiden name because of the children, which is a lot of bull. Her kids are away at private school, and she hardly ever sees them anyway. They come home about twice a year, and when she goes up there on Parents' Weekend she can be Baroness von Schmidt all she wants."

"Is she really a baroness?"

"Her ex-husband claimed he was a baron, if that's what you mean. Actually," Charlotte said with satisfaction, "we did manage to talk her into getting rid of her maid and hiring a cleaning service. There's nothing wrong with paying somebody to do the dirty work, but you just can't exploit a Third World sister. We tried to get the maid to join our group, but she wouldn't come."

Artificial topiary trees stuck up like lollipops from tubs on each side of the entrance to the pyramid. A coat of arms was painted on the door, and above it a lion's head held a brass ring in its mouth. Charlotte lifted the ring and let it fall with a clank. Immediately the door was flung open by a woman who looked as though the big joy in life was flinging open doors and maybe even practiced when nobody was around. She wore a long gown with full sleeves and a very low neckline. The gown was white with blue flowers the same color as her eyes and eye-shadow. Her blond hair was propped on top of her head with a comb, a few carefully arranged wisps escaping from it. Gold hoops the size of the one in the lion's mouth dangled from her ears.

"Darlings!" the door-opener cried, tossing her head so the hoops swayed and the wisps fluttered. "I'm Moozy," she said to me, "and you must be C.C."

Trailing a flowery perfume, Moozy led us down the hall, where we dropped our coats next to the marble bust of a curly-haired man with blank eyeballs and a stern mouth, and on into the living room. Huge portraits of a boy and a girl with candy-colored lips and cheeks hung above a sofa upholstered to match the eyes of the two kids and their mother. The little girl in the painting held a Siamese cat. A cat exactly like it sat on the back of the sofa, twitching the tip of its tail. There were, in fact, Siamese cats all around the room, looking like needlework pillows or china figurines or small throw rugs, depending on where and how they posed. One of them was cleaning itself on the lap of a woman in army surplus khakis who looked ready to start a workers' uprising. The rebel leader kept stroking the cat and nodding at a story being told by a woman in a pinstriped pants suit and shiny auburn wig. The lion's head clanked again, and Moozy swept off to fling open the door. Charlotte interrupted the pinstriped lady to introduce me. "C.C., Frances. Frances, C.C. C.C., Val. Val, C.C."

"Darlings!" we heard Moozy say.

There was room for one more person on the sofa, but I chose the floor next to the coffee table, which was loaded with food: hunks of cheese, platters of turkey and smoked ham, baskets of bread and crackers, bowls of nuts and fruit. There was also a silver tray with wine glasses on stems like threads and a couple of bottles labeled to show the wine was foreign and old. While the new arrivals all said hello, how are you, what's new, nothing much how about you?, I assembled a series of small sandwiches and lined them up on top of my thigh. "This last trip was fabulous, the best I've ever had, the high point of my career," Frances, the one in pinstripes, was saying for the third time.

Moozy poured wine for everybody, including me, and passed out the fragile glasses with graceful sweeps of her arm and jangles of her several bracelets. She smiled all the time, even when I shook my head no about the wine. Then she settled in a high-backed wing chair, first dislodging a cat, and arranged her long skirt and asked me to introduce myself formally, although everybody knew by then that I was Charlotte's niece.

My mouth was full of ham and crackers. "I'm C.C. Poindexter," I told them, spraying crumbs all over the Oriental rug. "The second C is for Charlotte, who is my aunt."

Moozy was nodding and smiling from ear to ear as

though I had just announced that I was of royal blood. One by one in order around the room, each person told me her name, which I instantly forgot, and said something about herself, most of it something humorous that I didn't get and wasn't supposed to.

"We're all just as pleased as can be that you-all have joined us tonight," Moozy said, thick as molasses. Her accent came and went between South Carolina and Long Island. "But won't you-all tell us something about yourself? Who you *are?* Where you are *goin'?*"

"I'm fifteen and a half and a sophomore in high school. And I'm not sure that I'm going much of anywhere." Which was more truth than I had intended, and I concentrated on picking up the cracker crumbs from the rug. My friend Laura knew exactly where she was going, but I didn't have the vaguest idea, not back then. No special interests, no special talents. My mother said there was no sense worrying about it, because some man would probably come along and change whatever plans I made anyway (although she was also afraid he might not, since I was so tall), and that I should concentrate on being a nice person and learn typing and shorthand which was still the best way to get a job, college degree or not.

That confession hit Moozy like a sack of grits. She set her wine glass down on a bowlegged table and leaned back, eyes closed, pinching the bridge of her nose. She was no longer smiling. "I had intended," she said slowly, "to ask tonight for a discussion of women and the problem of credit, but I think we've got a rare and valuable opportunity here. C.C. is a young sister at the crossroads, the first of *many* crossroads in her life, and we've got a chance, a very rare and precious chance, to help her look deeper into herself." Moozy's voice wound itself higher and tighter. A cat stretched and rubbed against her leg, and she reached down to stroke it, eyes still closed. "This evening may be the turning point in C.C.'s young life. It could be crucial. Critical, even. Maybe a matter of life and death, symbolically if not literally." She opened her eyes and focused on me from under the awnings of her false eyelashes. "C.C., dear, would it be all right with you if we explored goals and values with you tonight?"

There were nine women in the room, and they were all looking at me. Charlotte had told me they had been through a lot together since the group had started: separation, divorce, reconciliation, abortion, career change, hassles with kids on drugs—"the usual women problems," she had said. They were good at problems, because they had so many. And now they had me.

"You can say no if you want to," Charlotte said, those concerned frown lines between her eyes, "but I think it would be a terrific growth experience for you."

So I nodded and answered sure, yeah, okay, all the time wishing I had said I wanted to be a steeplejack, or at least had the basic guts to tell them to keep their noses pointed toward their own goals.

Frances took over. But first she gave a little speech. "I've been using values clarification techniques, which were so successful when we experimented with them two weeks ago at my place—in fact I think the last meeting was unquestionably the best this group has ever had." She looked around to see if anybody was going to challenge that statement; her tone made you know you could not even *wonder* if she might be wrong, let alone disagree with her out loud. "I've been using them in my business semi-

15

nars with enormous success; I'm always being asked to do them, more requests than I can handle, and I think once C.C. has worked through a couple of these exercises we'll have a clearer picture of where she is now, after which we can help her see where she ought to go."

She handed me a clipboard with a sheet of yellow legal paper headed, in Frances's almost unreadable script, *Twenty Things You Enjoy Doing Most*. Numbers from one to twenty ran down the left margin. She also gave me a file card with the special codings. After I had the list made, I was supposed to pick out the five best things and number them in order, and then mark the ones I liked to do alone, and next the ones I liked to do with other people, and the ones I wouldn't have had on my list five years ago, and so on. It was terribly complicated.

Having given me the assignment, they turned their attention to other things. Themselves. Thank goodness.

"Michael invited me to come down and visit his commune," Charlotte reported, while I retraced the twenty numbers with Frances's initialed gold pen to make sure they were clear.

"How simply marvelous," Moozy twittered.

Frances didn't think it was marvelous. "If I were you," Frances advised firmly, "I'd insist that Michael come back to see you first, to apologize. Why should you go through all that, after the worry and pain he's caused you? Typical male: jump when I whistle."

I wrote down beside number one on the list, "Living on a commune," because I was pretty sure I'd like it, even though I had never even thought of it before.

Then Rosaria, a pretty woman with a Spanish accent, said children behaved toward their parents the way they did because of their early training, and she personally was disturbed because her own children wouldn't go to mass on Sundays.

Frances cut her short. "But the church is just another sexist institution. Why would you want them to go? What chance does your daughter have of becoming a priest?"

I wrote, "Going on picnics" next, because I remembered when we lived in another town years ago that I liked to go to the Sunday School picnics, even though I didn't like the Sunday School.

Val, the woman in khaki, said, "My father was a Methodist minister, out in Kansas you know, so I grew up as a p.k.—preacher's kid. Certain things were expected of a girl p.k. that weren't expected of my brothers." And then she told about the time she had run away from home because she had been forbidden to ride bareback, which nice girls didn't do. Especially p.k.'s.

I added "Riding horseback," which I had done on two separate occasions when our family went on vacation in Pennsylvania. I don't think it was bareback. I'm sure there was a saddle that I hung onto.

Then Frances told a story about the time *she* ran away from home and convinced a bus driver to take her all the way to Madison, Wisconsin. Frances spoke as though she were addressing an auditorium full of people, and everyone laughed even though it didn't have a thing to do with the problems of the woman who wanted her children to go to church, or even with riding bareback.

But it was Linda who finally caught and held the group's attention. I remembered her name easily because she looked so much like my mother. She wore big round glasses with thick lenses, and her longish brown hair had a streak of gray on one side. Her short skirt kept hiking up about fourteen inches above her knees and exposing her not very terrific thighs. "I've met somebody," she announced very quietly.

Moozy vaulted out of her wing chair. "Wait, wait, don't start your story yet," she commanded, and she fluttered around refilling everybody's wine glass. I added "Going to movies" and "Walking on the beach" to my list. Moozy settled down again and laced her fingers. "Now," she said, "tell us about him."

Linda narrated her tale about the new man in her life—when and how they met, what he said, what she said, and so on—the way Ernest Hemingway wrote about big game hunting in Africa, all very quiet but tense so you could smell the danger. This was a Big One. I fixed myself a few more cracker sandwiches and wrote "Cooking" on my list, a gross exaggeration.

"I know that one," my aunt cut in. "Can't be trusted." Just like a renegade elephant.

Linda's big glasses kept slipping and she kept pushing them back up with one finger. "Well, just which ones *can* you trust? We all know what they're like."

The other rappers cross-examined Linda about her man, but when they asked a question it seemed it was mainly so they could tell a story of their own. "Exactly what did he say when he asked you to go away for the weekend?" Val wanted to know. "Because when that guy Walter invited me to go with him on his sailboat in the Bahamas, he never once mentioned that he had a wife who got seasick."

I put down "Sailing." Just before my father moved out we had been planning to go to a lake in New Hampshire on a family vacation, and he had promised to take me sailing. But as it turned out he went to New Hampshire alone, saying he would take my sister and me the next time. I have still never been on a sailboat.

Linda heaved up her shoulders in an exaggerated shrug and her glasses slipped again. "He's a good lover."

Everyone applauded. Linda grinned down at her lap and pushed up her glasses.

"When you've managed to separate the elements, to take what's good and to ignore what's bad, then you're really in control," Frances announced.

"Expecting love and romance in every relationship is what gets us all into trouble," said my aunt, as though she were reading from a manual.

I wrote "Making love," which is what my mother calls it, and crossed it out because that is not the term used by any of the kids I know or by liberated women either, but I couldn't quite bring myself to write what we actually say. Saying something is a lot different from writing it. Finally I crossed that out and wrote instead "Sex." Then I quickly added several other things to the list after it, like "Reading poetry" and "Listening to records," so that sex would not be so noticeable.

The problem was that I was supposed to mark each item on my list with "date you last enjoyed it," which in the case of listening to records was yesterday and in the case of sailing and sex, never. I was still a virgin and probably always would be at the rate I was going, being so much taller than all the boys I knew, destined to think about the eighth item on my list for the rest of my life but never to do it.

There was a sudden silence among the rappers when

they remembered that a child, me, was present. They didn't want a fifteen-year-old to be *that* liberated. Moozy said, "Well, C.C., how's the list coming along?"

"I've only got thirteen items. I can't think of any more."

Frances frowned. "I suppose that's enough to give us an indication. . . . How would you feel about reading it off to us, so we can all get the profile at the same time?"

"Don't feel shy with us, darling," Moozy said. "We're a very loving and sharing group."

So I read the list, being careful not to change my voice or anything when I mentioned sex in between sailing and reading poetry. They didn't ask for the codings, so the fact that some of the items were strictly imaginary wasn't even noticed. When I finished I could see Charlotte staring at me with this funny expression, surprise and puzzlement and worry, all of which she was trying not to show. It was worth it, just to see the look on her face. I knew I was going to hear more about this. I just hoped it wasn't going to be one of the rare things my aunt ever discussed with my mother.

They analyzed my list almost as though I wasn't there. They worried that cooking might show I had accepted a traditional definition of a woman's role. They were glad that I enjoyed the outdoors, on picnics and horseback and sailboats. They decided, since I said I like to do a lot of things alone, that I was a loner. They concluded that I was an individual, and they ignored sex completely.

Then Linda asked me, "Whom do you most admire?"

I started to say my father, which was true even though I sometimes hated him for leaving. And I really admired my aunt, too, but it would have sounded weird to say so right then. So I said, because I had just read about her in one of my mother's magazines, "Mrs. Henry Kissinger."

That got more of a reaction than anything on my list.

"But whatever for, love?" Moozy asked in her southernmost accent.

And since I didn't know how to back out of it I mumbled the truth: "Because she's tall and she's married to somebody important who is shorter than she is and neither of them seems to care."

"Wow, do you need to have your consciousness raised!" said Linda, who was not anywhere near six feet tall and did not have to invent stuff to put on her "Things I Enjoy Doing Most" list because she was probably already doing them with her new boyfriend, even though she has flabby thighs with blue lines.

They all had a lot of advice on how to be proud of my own attributes. The Spanish woman said what pretty eyes I have (greenish brown like my aunt's and my father's) and how men are usually more attracted by a nice pair of eyes than they are by big breasts. What she didn't realize is that most of the boys I know don't see much above my chin when I'm standing up. Then Frances said this was the wrong thing to be telling me, that the point is to be able to get along without men, period.

And then they all began talking about whether men are necessary.

While they were discussing the pros and cons of men, Charlotte picked up a bright green silk pillow from the sofa and set it against a sliver of wall beside a grandfather's clock and eased into a yoga handstand. She kept on with the discussion upside down. My aunt believes that men are both necessary and desirable. Frances does not. Moozy is for men; Val is not. Linda is for, and Rosaria and the rest were undecided. Charlotte came down off the wall, her face flushed.

After a while Frances said she had to catch a plane early the next morning. That was the signal for everybody to leave. Val reminded them it was her turn to have the next rap session. Moozy thanked everybody for coming, especially me, and said she hoped they had been of help. Frances said she would be glad to work with me on more values clarification if I wanted. Finally Charlotte and I climbed into the van and started home.

We hadn't even cleared the gates of Les Artistes when Charlotte said, "Oh, C.C., listen, uh, I hope you're protecting yourself?"

"I've got my seatbelt on," I said. I knew what she was talking about, but it seemed like more fun to play dumb. Playing dumb is one of the things I'm good at.

"From getting pregnant, idiot!"

"Oh" was all I said. I could tell she was getting really irritated from the way she took the van around a corner.

"Well, *are* you?"

"I'm not pregnant. Not to the best of my knowledge."

She was exasperated; this was serious stuff. "Cynthia Charlotte Poindexter, exactly what precautions are you taking to keep from getting pregnant?"

"An absolutely foolproof one." I decided out of pure stubbornness not to tell her that my method was total abstinence reinforced by total lack of opportunity.

She humphed. We were in heavy traffic with lots of potential red lights, and it was a bad time to be tackling such a tough subject.

"I rather doubt that," she said. "I think I'd better take you to my doctor for a checkup. Then she can decide whether you ought to be on the pill or get a loop. And don't worry—she won't say anything to Margaret about this. And you can be sure I wouldn't."

"Ummm." Maybe I ought to do it anyway, I thought. Just in case my fortunes change suddenly and somebody falls passionately in love with me. But at the same time I wasn't sure I wanted to go to bed with anybody, even if he loved me passionately and was four inches taller than me and I loved him passionately back. Laura and I discussed it often, but never with the same conclusions. Anyway, I wouldn't accept Charlotte's offer until I had talked it over with Laura. So much for being a loner.

"When are you going down to Virginia to see Michael?"

"You're not very subtle about changing the subject. I'm probably going to go next month over spring vacation."

"Is it really okay if I go too?"

"I wouldn't have suggested it if I hadn't meant it."

We had reached the thruway. Charlotte urged the van out into the first lane of traffic and then left into the center lane, square in front of a tractor-trailer rig. The driver leaned on his horn, and we both jumped. Charlotte settled down in the middle lane, the truck tailgating. "All I can see is that creep's grille," she said, keeping the van exactly on the speed limit. "He's not allowed to pass on the left, and he doesn't want to drive in the right lane either. Let him move. Damned if I will."

The battle was on. The truck driver kept blasting his horn and easing up almost close enough to touch, air brakes hissing. Finally he swung his rig into the illegal left lane, still blasting and yelling at Charlotte. I couldn't make out what he said, but I could pretty much guess. He made an obscene gesture and my aunt joyfully made one back. She almost missed our exit, she was enjoying the fight so much.

Lights were shining at the end of our driveway, by the kitchen door, in the downstairs hall, and back in my mother's bedroom. The living room was dark. We hardly ever used it after my father moved out.

All the way home I had been trying to work out a reasonable strategy for asking her if I could go to Virginia with Charlotte, and then I got mad because it seemed to me I shouldn't have to have a strategy. I should be able to make a reasonable request and get a positive answer. Or at least a reasonable answer. For a while I thought how much easier life would be if I were Charlotte's daughter. The idea kept banging around in my head that maybe I could live with her anyway, even if we weren't mother and daughter. My mother got along much better with my sister Allison, so she wouldn't be lonely. My mother was probably right that Charlotte was not the kind of mother Michael needed, but I don't believe she ever thought that *she* was not the kind of mother *I* needed. It was almost as though my crib and Michael's had been mixed up in the hospital nursery.

"I've got bad feelings about what Mom will say about Wisdom Peak," I said.

"Damn. I should have checked your chart before we left. Transiting planets can give you a pretty good idea of what to expect in situations like this. But listen, there's no big rush. Let it go for a while, and I'll look up your chart and see what the indications are. Keep cool. It'll work out."

She drove away and I went inside to check in with my mother, who was lying in bed propped on one elbow with a book open beside her. She seemed to be going to bed earlier and earlier.

"You're out late for a school night," Mom said, anger registering at about three on a scale of one to ten, so I stayed in the doorway instead of going in to sit on her bed. "How was the rap session?"

"Pretty good. Moozy is a baroness. Or she was when she was married to the baron. Her accent is sort of southern. You'd like her house, though," I rattled on, trying to think of positive things to say.

"What did they rap about?"

"Oh, I don't know. Lots of things. Whether children should be forced to go to church or not."

"A whole evening on that?"

"Charlotte was telling them about Michael and how he wants her to come there to his commune for a visit over spring vacation." I said it because it is my nature to ignore good advice and ask for trouble.

"Is she going?"

"Yeah, I guess she is."

"She's nuts!" my mother said, slapping shut her book for emphasis. "I hope you don't ever get any loony ideas about communes. Any parent who lets a child go off to live like that ought to have her or his head examined."

I worked at scraping some dirt from under a fingernail. "Charlotte says Michael's really happy there. They have a very efficient organization and everybody has work to do. It's not like those places where nobody has to do anything."

"Your *Aunt* Charlotte is hardly the person I'd accept

25

as an authority on the subject of children's happiness." She opened her book again.

I said good night and went upstairs to wash my hair, which I often do in times of stress. With a towel wrapped around my head I crept down into the kitchen and started to dial Charlotte's number. Then I remembered that Charlotte rarely answers her phone anyway, so I hung up again. I really didn't need any astrological charts to tell me the situation was *bad*.

Chapter Two

 The flabby strands of spaghetti were too short to spin on a fork. They lay in puddles of sauce like limp string in red glue, which we coated with a layer of sawdust that smelled faintly parmesan. This was how we knew that it was Wednesday, and that we were in the Greenfield High School cafeteria.

"It takes imagination to produce food this bad," my friend Laura said. "What's worse is stuff like frozen dinners which pretend to be good. This is an art form that does not pretend to be anything but totally awful. Tomorrow's leaders are being nourished by this babalooey."

"Maybe we should revolt," I suggested. "If nobody ate it, they'd have to do something about it."

"Terrible food is our inalienable right," Laura said, scooping it in with a soup spoon as though she really enjoyed it. Laura has a weight problem. She'll eat absolutely anything, whether she thinks it's good or not. "Remember in elementary school when it was a status thing to bring hot lunch money every Monday? We felt superior to the kids who brown-bagged Velveeta or Skippy sandwiches or even rare roast beef. And how in middle school we actually connived for seconds on pseudo-pizza and sloppy joes? And by the time we got to high school we were addicted. It's a conspiracy, you know, to keep the student body submissive."

"Yeah, but who's the brains behind it? Who gives the orders to the gray-haired ladies with fuzzy chins back in the kitchen?" I was working my way through a bowl of brown-edged lettuce swimming in greasy vinegar, listed on the menu board as Crispy Tossed Green Salad with Herb Dressing.

"It's our fate." Laura sighed. "Who could dream of revolting against such a clever system?"

"I got to be six foot one eating this food," I said.

"And I got to weigh a hundred and sixty-eight pounds." She kept right on eating.

"I went to Charlotte's rap group last night," I announced, to get her away from thinking about fat.

"Really? What was it like?"

I told her about Baroness Moozy and the other rappers and the values clarification ordeal. Laura said it was a good story, even though she was not much interested in the women's movement. Her mother had always been liberated, Laura said, and if Laura or her mother had their consciousnesses raised any higher they'd get nosebleeds. She didn't need to have her values clarified, either.

Laura had her life completely planned from the day she started sixth grade: she would go to Princeton to major in sociology, and then to Harvard to get a masters in Business Administration, and then to Columbia for a law degree. When she is thirty she intends to marry a man who is looking for the same thing she is—an interdependent relationship in which there will be mutual support but complete freedom. No children.

"My cousin Michael invited Charlotte to go to Wisdom Peak for a visit." That set her up for the real news: "She says I can go along with her over spring vacation."

Laura, who usually goes to an island in the Caribbean over spring vacation, turned a satisfying green. "Sounds like an interesting experience," she said.

"I'm not sure my mother will let me."

Laura skewed her face. "Margaret does have a problem letting go, doesn't she? But don't worry. I'll work on this."

Laura and I were counting the cherries in our Sparkling Fruited Jello with Fluffy Whipped Topping and nursing a second container of warmish milk when Karen Miller eased past our seats. Laura said hello twice before Karen even noticed her, nodded, and sat down alone two tables over. "Have you heard about the Miller Situation?" Laura whispered. "That brings it to thirty-seven percent."

In her desk at home Laura had a black ledger book in which she kept track of the separations, divorces, and remarriages among parents of people she knew. The Miller Situation was probably already entered in columns under the headings Laura had set up: family name, names of husband, wife, children; notes about personality of each; date of separation, custody of children, probable causes of breakup, adjustment of family members, and a broad column called "Remarks."

At first the ledger was very neat and orderly, "unlike the lives of the people recorded in it," according to Laura.

But then she got carried away. She set up a page for every family she could think of, no matter what their status, added a column for Conflicts and another one with pluses and minuses—her "gut reaction" for whether or not the family would survive intact. It really bothered her when a family stayed together in spite of her predictions, or when there was a split she hadn't foreseen.

While we dumped our garbage, Laura reviewed the Miller Situation. "Obviously incompatible people," she said. "I've had that family on minus from the very beginning." We clattered our trays onto the cleanup carts and started toward our classrooms. "I predict that Dr. Miller will marry his nurse within a year and that Karen will not like his new wife and will go to live with her mother, even if it does mean changing schools in her senior year, because she does not have the courage to run away with Sammy Lewis."

I am the only other person to have seen Laura's ledger. Under the entry for her own parents, MONTGOMERY —Fred & Lois—there were only sparse notes. They were not only still married but were partners in an architectural firm and seemed to like each other. Laura could find no signs of decay in her parents' marriage. She gave them a plus, but she still wasn't satisfied.

"Sometimes," Laura said with a soul-sigh, "I wish my parents had some *passion*. Like the Reisses."

Wendy Reiss's family had lived in our neighborhood for about eighteen months, the usual length of time that executives are allowed to stay before they are transferred somewhere else, a system that Laura says is used to keep them in line. The Reisses separated and reconciled three times while they lived in Greenfield. Once Mrs. Reiss had gone to a Parents Association meeting with dark glasses on, and everyone knew that she had a black eye because Mr. Reiss had thrown a book at her and she had not ducked. We knew from Wendy, who always talked about such things. Then her parents went to Bermuda for five days to make up. Laura had given them a plus when they moved to Michigan. Passionate people, she said, tend to stay together.

When the column labeled Remarks got too crowded, Laura set up a system of five by seven file cards on which she made additional notes, what she observed and what she imagined (she called it "deduced"). The Poindexter family saga already filled both sides of two cards and part of a third, because I told her too much. Those cards were beginning to be a problem between us. I knew every time I told her something she rushed home to make a note on our card. One thing about the Miller Situation was that it gave her something to think about besides the Poindexters.

The Poindexter Situation was one of the early entries in the ledger. I once asked Laura if I could read it, and she said I could. She's a very frank person, and sometimes I wish she were not. She handed me the book, open to the right page.

POINDEXTER—Jack & Margaret
husb: late 40s, tall, gd phys cond., attrac to women
wife: abt 40, fair shape for age, quiet, conserv, dependent
children: CC, 15, 6'1" tall, intell but lacks direc, selfcons; Allison, 10, cute, spoiled, loud
reason: husb's adolescent yearning for freedom

The only date mentioned was July 5, a year ago, when Dad moved out. But under Remarks Laura got completely torqued: "CC and Marg haven't accept sit. Marg reclusive and bitter. CC has add'tl probs of rejec due to abnml ht. Therapy indicated."

"Therapy for *what?*" I had bellowed. "To make me shorter?"

"To make you accepting," she had answered calmly.

Laura frequently says infuriating things like that. In spite of it, we are best friends. Laura has an I.Q. of something phenomenal, and she started taking accelerated programs and enrichment courses practically in kindergarten. Which meant the only classes we have together are phys ed, in which we are both complete flabs. Nobody expects much physical from a brain like Laura, but it is a tremendous disappointment to the teacher that anybody as tall as I am can't seem to hit the basket any way but accidentally.

I walked Laura to her Advanced Statistics class. We still had three minutes until the bell, time we normally kill by the door since my study hall is in the next room. Then Laura looked in and saw that Mr. Hayes, the teacher, was not at his desk. In his place sat the substitute, Mr. McDermott. Laura was insanely in love with Philip McDermott. So were at least eleven other girls I can name, and possibly a few teachers. Mr. McDermott had a thick black beard and wore jeans and tennis shoes and rode a motor scooter. Laura said his brown eyes were "gypsy-like" and "broodingly mysterious."

Mr. McDermott is a poet. He substituted in practically any class where he was needed, since poets have a hard time finding steady work. Unless the teacher left a lesson plan or some exercises for the students to do, he made it a poetry class. Even auto shop, where he once had all the guys writing poems about their cars. They were too surprised to resist.

Laura naturally managed to find out a lot about him: that he had studied at the Sorbonne and worked for a construction company in Marrakech and built a boat which he sailed to Tenerife in the Canary Islands, where he lived in a hut overlooking the sea and wrote poetry for a year. She said he was twenty-nine. He told her.

He is missing the first knuckle of the index finger of his left hand. Sue Brodie, who was also in love with him, said he told her it was bitten off by a shark when he was living in Yucatan. Laura claimed it was an accident in a logging camp in British Columbia. Sue said Mr. McDermott told her he was thirty-five. No one knew for sure if he was married, but we all assumed he was not. Poets aren't, usually.

"Do you know Mr. McDermott?" I once asked Charlotte.

"Everybody knows Fabulous Phil," she said. "Actually fabulous isn't the word I'd use, but it does start with an F."

"Laura is in love with him."

"About half the females in this school are in love with him."

"Including you?"

"McDermott is a male chauvinist poet," she said in an ironic tone.

Laura rushed into her statistics class as though I didn't exist. "See you after school," I called after her.

When we met by my locker after our last class, Laura was high on poetry.

"He got us to write poems on the subject of probability. You know—when you flip a coin, whether it's going to be heads or tails, and how this works out in life. It was just beautiful! And he said that he doesn't even know how to balance a checkbook, he doesn't *believe* in such things

33

as checkbooks, but he knows all about Pascal, the French philosopher who developed the whole theory of probability, you know, and he told us about Pascal's philosophy and the inadequacy of reason and how he believes the poet has to take over where the statistician leaves off for true understanding."

All this while we were walking home from school. It was a very one-sided conversation.

We did not ride the school bus, because in order to qualify for a bus pass you have to live at least one point five miles from school. We both lived one point forty-nine miles away, although our houses were six-tenths of a mile apart. In the morning I walked to her house, and we went to school together from there. In the afternoon we walked to my house, and then she went the rest of the way by herself. It took Laura most of the one point forty-nine miles to tell me everything that Mr. McDermott said and did in statistics class, while I tried to make intelligent noises and not appear bored.

We started up the driveway to my house, Laura still on poetry but ready to forage in our kitchen. Then I remembered: "My mother is having company tonight," I told her. "I don't think it's a good time to stop in."

"So why don't you come over to my house to eat tonight? Fred and Lois are both away. I'll read you my probability poem."

We shook hands, a new thing Laura started since she came back from spending the Christmas vacation in Europe. I promised to be there at six. That gave me three hours to study, most of which I would spend reading books that had not been assigned and listening to loud music that my mother loathes, hates, and despises. It would give

Laura, who seems not to need to study, ever, for anything, three hours to work on the Miller Situation and Mr. Mc-Dermott and Pascal.

My mother had rearranged all the furniture in the living room. The big pieces were pushed back against the walls, and the dining room chairs were stuck in the empty spaces. It looked stiff and cold. Mom was in the kitchen, filling a big coffee urn with water.

"Hi." The chair where I always drop my books and jacket wasn't there.

"Hi. Good day? Take your things up to your room. I'm trying to keep this place neat."

"Yessum. Which group is coming tonight?" I opened the refrigerator and pulled out a big chunk of cheese, some leftover meatloaf, and a jug of milk.

"As I told you this morning, and yesterday when Gloria Panek brought the urn, and last week when it was planned, it's the Contemporary Literature Group. And don't eat that cheese. I need it for something."

She was in her usual constipated mood. I tried to remember what she was like five years ago, when I was Allison's age, and I didn't know if *she* had changed so much or if *I* had. When Dad was here, I just avoided her when her moods were rocky. But after he left it got harder.

Dad had been gone for almost six months before Mom started going out anywhere except to the Andersons' on the other side of the street and down three houses. At first Mrs. Anderson invited her over for dinner often, but then she stopped. Mom couldn't figure out why, but Laura's opinion was that Mrs. Anderson was very jealous of Mr. Anderson, because she was a basically insecure woman, and my mother seemed threatening—that she might take Mr.

Anderson away. I thought that was funny, because I knew that Mom didn't even like Mr. Anderson much at all and only kept up the friendship in the first place because she had known Mrs. Anderson for years and needed to see people once in a while.

Charlotte tried to get Mom to join the rap group, or to take a yoga class, or to enroll in psychodrama or bio-energetics, but my mother did not believe in any of those things and always said politely, "No thank you." Charlotte gave up and said she'd just have to work things out for herself.

Then a couple of months later she joined a club for divorced people called Encore Singles. Charlotte said it was a stage a lot of people went through when they thought remarriage would solve all their problems, because essentially it was an organization for finding you a new mate. She said once you got over the desperation of the hunt, it was generally harmless.

Encore Singles certainly had plenty for their members to do. I looked through the monthly newsletter that Mom got. You could join a Ping-Pong group, a tennis group, a folk dance group, a choral group, a classical guitar group, a group for going to plays and a group for writing and reading poetry. There were groups for classical music and rock music. You could join groups to learn to refinish furniture, figure skate, take pictures, play bridge, and paint in watercolors. They scheduled trips with the kids to the Museum of Natural History, to ski resorts in Vermont and camp-outs in the Berkshires. There were Adults Only trips to Mexico and Las Vegas. There were pool parties and breakfast-on-the-beach parties and dances every Friday night. On Sunday evenings serious discussion groups met to explore topics like "Am I Capable of Loving Again?" It was hard to think of anything Encore Singles didn't offer.

Mrs. Panek, whom my mother knew only slightly before she was divorced but got to know much better afterward (Mrs. Panek is divorced too), persuaded her to join. She talked her first into going to one of the Friday night dances. My mother put her hair on rollers and applied a little subtle makeup. She dressed up in a dark red silk dress she had made from a designer pattern. It had a high round neck and long sleeves, and she wore my great-grandmother's pearl pin. When she combed her hair out it was full and soft around her face instead of pulled straight back the way she usually wore it.

Mrs. Panek came to pick her up. Her long black dress fitted like paint. It was slit up the front and down the neck and had silver threads in it that shimmered when she walked. Mrs. Panek wore a silver wig and turquoise eye shadow. I hardly recognized her. My mother stared, and she stared back at my mother.

"Honey," Mrs. Panek said, "you really do look sweet and pretty. But you don't look sexy, and that's the name of the game at the Friday night dances."

I could see that my mother wanted to call the whole thing off. "I don't own anything sexy," she said, and went bravely forth in her plain, long-sleeved dress that I had watched her sew.

I was still up listening to records when she came home. Most of the curl was gone from her hair, and it straggled down around her neck. "Gloria Panek was absolutely right. But this is obviously not my game. I'd rather go to bed early with a good book than go through *that* again."

For a while that's what she did. Then somebody in charge of getting new members involved in activities called and asked her if the Contemporary Literature Group could meet at our house. The first time she said no and the second time she said no, but the third time she gave in and borrowed Mrs. Panek's twenty-cup coffee maker and baked a chocolate bundt cake and rearranged the furniture and reread two Kurt Vonnegut novels to prepare for the group, which was due to arrive at our house that night.

"Okay if I eat supper at Laura's?"

"Mmm. But don't stay late." She was measuring scoops of coffee into the top of the urn.

"Expecting a big crowd?"

"They told me it varies. Better be ready for about fifteen."

"Save me some cake, if you can."

I helped her set out plates and cups and silverware on the dining room table and wiped up the powder room. Then I went upstairs to do my biology and history homework. But mostly I lay on my French Provincial canopy bed and tried to visualize how the room would look with an Indian print bedspread hooked up to the ceiling and more bedspreads hung around the walls so it would be like the inside of an exotic tent. At a quarter of six I left for Laura's.

Laura's house was all angles. Her parents designed it so there was no free-standing furniture. Everything was built in. If her mother would for some reason be having the Encore Singles Contemporary Literature Group, there would be no chairs to lug around. Everyone would just find a place among the hundreds of pillows on the long bench that ran all around the room, zigging and zagging with the angles. The carpet went right up over the bench and continued on up the wall.

Laura's room had a sleeping unit with pull-out space for an overnight guest and a storage unit with drawers and separate compartments for storing each kind of item: skirts one place, jeans another, and so on. But Laura just stuffed everything in wherever it was handy. There was a recreation unit with special surfaces that folded out for playing games or for working on hobbies, with cubicles for collections of rocks, seashells, etc. The cubicles were mostly empty or crammed with miscellaneous junk, because the only things Laura collected on purpose were data and statistics, which required only her ledger and file cards. Her study unit had a seat designed for the most alert posture, and the built-in lighting was arranged so the light would fall on books and papers at the correct angle. But Laura always read in bed with a flashlight, because the lights above the sleeping unit were very soft and diffused.

Mildred, the Montgomerys' housekeeper, was in the kitchen when I arrived. Mildred did not cook, and she did not like anyone to be in the kitchen who did. There was a regular oven big enough to roast a witch, a microwave oven, a stainless steel range with six burners and a hood, and a double refrigerator. Laura had explained that the kitchen was designed so they could hire a cook and entertain clients at home, but they were never able to find the right person to use it all. Mildred said she was a "plain cook," which meant that she knew how to turn out meatloaf and fried potatoes, but not boeuf bourguignon or veal Cordon Bleu, which is what the Montgomerys had in mind. But they were glad to get somebody who could keep a house in order in this servantless day and age. Charlotte disapproved of Lois Montgomery's philosophy; she felt Lois should simplify her life so that she did not require the services of another woman to keep it running smoothly.

Mildred had a strange personality. Laura considered her an interesting case, but she made me feel uncomfortable, as though I had just made a mess on the gleaming tile floor. Mildred never smiled, but she threw her head back and laughed gleefully—"hee hee hee"—when something bad happened: a wreck on the thruway, a fire with extensive property damage and loss of life, a high-voltage short that executed at least one lineman, a child suffering from a rare and incurable disease. When something good happened (I can't think of any examples), Mildred became sullen and mopey.

Laura, brazening past Mildred, had planned our dinner. Out of the freezer and into the microwave oven went two quiches lorraines, which her mother bought regularly from a catering service. From the pantry cupboard came one small jar of caviar, one box of crackers imported from Japan, one tin of smoked oysters, and one can of Greek olives.

"Looks good, except for the olives."

"I'll eat them," Laura promised.

Mildred glowered at us over her newspaper, watching to make sure we cleaned up after ourselves. She was not paid, she said, to clean up after a couple of spoiled brats. Laura ignored her, arranging plates and silverware on separate trays.

We went into the entertainment center to watch television until the quiches were ready. Laura slid open the panel in front of the concealed TV and flicked it on to a late afternoon movie in which a woman in a ruffled apron put down her dishtowel and rushed to open the door for a man in a large hat. He dropped his hat next to her dishtowel and picked her up and swung her around while they both grinned like fools and stared into each other's eyes.

"This is what's wrong, of course," said Laura. "The expectations of our parents' generation were formed by this kind of babalooey. When they married, they thought it was going to be like this: kissing in the kitchen. As my figures show, it doesn't work."

A bell rang, and I followed Laura into the kitchen to get our quiches out of the oven. Mildred sat at the counter, thumbing the pages of a newspaper that specializes in news of dismembered babies. She was chuckling to herself. I tried to imagine Mildred in a ruffled apron being swooped around by a man in a large hat.

"Where are your parents?" I asked Laura. Mildred chuckled again.

"Lois is in the Bahamas, designing a cottage colony, and Fred is in Ohio, doing I forget what. Maybe that's the library job."

"Maine," said Mildred.

"No, I'm sure he said Ohio."

"Maine," Mildred repeated.

"Fred is in *Ohio*," Laura told her firmly.

Mildred threw her head back and laughed. I could see the fillings in her molars, and her laugh screeched up and down my spine.

We carried our trays with the quiches back to the entertainment center. From a small concealed refrigerator next to the concealed television Laura produced two cans of grape soda. In unison we pulled the rings on the tops of the cans and dropped them through the openings into the soda. We drank a silent toast to each other and to ourselves. The couple on television was arguing. The woman began to cry into her apron. The man stalked angrily away and then came back and comforted her. She sobbed a couple of times and smiled up at him. He kissed her. "Babalooey!" Laura shouted at the screen.

"But it's what everybody dreams of," I told her, keeping a straight face and watching her grab for the bait.

"And that's exactly what's wrong. The dreams are pure babalooey. And to expect that sort of thing can lead only to disappointment. Now in an equal and interdependent relationship—"

"But don't you want some of those things too? I mean, wouldn't it be nice to have somebody—Philip McDermott, say—come into the kitchen, right now, and swing you around and kiss you like that?"

"The less you want and need of such things, the better off you are," Laura lectured me sternly. "Strip everything down to the bare essentials. And not just things. Emotions, too. For instance, my parents don't expect romance from each other. They are completely free. Lois goes to the Bahamas, Fred goes to Ohio—"

"Mildred says Maine."

She frowned. "She is thinking of another time. And they have separate friends and nobody asks any questions. Lois says that's what keeps the bloom on the rose. You know, keeps the romance alive."

"You just said they didn't expect romance. And you used to say you wished they had some passion." She was my best friend, probably my only friend, but I couldn't resist needling her when her smugness got to be too much to stand.

I had gotten to her, and she was annoyed. She changed the subject. "Want anything else to eat?" Without waiting for an answer, knowing what it would be, she located some cream-filled Twinkies in the back of the freezer. They were her favorite junk dessert. We watched the rest of the movie, which ended happily, and the news, which didn't, followed by a stupid game show.

"Guess I'd better head on home," I said, but I stayed to watch a special with a beautiful woman who sang and acted in skits but mostly moved around looking gorgeous in fantastic clothes. We stared at it all in unspeakable envy. Then I got up to leave.

"Have one for the road." I shoved another Twinkie in my jacket pocket and started down the Montgomerys' long, curved driveway with lights discreetly planted in the shrubbery.

The six-tenths of a mile of Pumpkin Stem Lane was dark, except for lights in the houses. Every light was blazing at our house, and six cars were lined up in the driveway with two more parked on the road, their wheels partly up on the grass. In the living room sat seven very neatly dressed women, all about my mother's age. There were also two men: one tall and stooped and bald, and one short and paunchy and bald. The short one had a raspy voice, and all the women laughed at everything he said. I thought I'd hang around and listen for a while, because I was sort of into Vonnegut, but nobody was talking about Vonnegut or about any kind of Contemporary Literature. They were discussing where they had been or were planning to go on vacation, and whether it was a swinging place to be or not.

So I drifted out to the kitchen where there was a big

chocolate cake on the counter with only a couple of pieces cut out of it. I figured all the women were probably on diets. While I was notching out a chunk, the short bald man came in with his coffee cup. He stopped, looked me up and down, grinned a froggy grin above his bow tie, and rasped, "Hiya, Stretch, how's the weather up there?"

I coolly flipped the cake into the palm of my hand and thought briefly about pushing it right into his grin. But I snapped back, "Why don't you grow up and find out?" And I carried my cake up to my room, stepped over the pile of dirty clothes by the door, and sat down on my unmade bed to consider my mother's fate, which didn't look much more promising than mine. Being middle-aged is possibly at least as bad as being tall.

Chapter Three

Three uneventful weeks later, on the evening of an otherwise uneventful Thursday, the phone rang. The phone was never for me. I let it ring and contemplated the mess in my room.

I am one of the few people I know of my age who do not have a phone in their room. My parents once promised me a telephone for my sixteenth birthday, but it turned out to be something I didn't really want. Laura and I had agreed never to call each other, except in dire emergency, because Laura is slightly paranoid and believed her line was being tapped because of her parents' ultra-leftwing political views. Charlotte never called either. She believes in face-to-face communication, because she says you give two messages, one with your voice and one with your body, and the body message is the one you really mean. She also says that the telephone is an intrusion on peace of mind and an invasion of privacy. When she was meditating or painting or reading or even just sitting there drinking tea, she usually refused to answer. "Eventually," she said, "people learn to leave you alone."

My mother used the phone all the time. She said it was her connection with the outside world. She would have liked a phone in every room, but as it was she still usually managed to answer on the second ring. But then my sister Allison started to get calls from all her silly friends, and they began calling up boys and giggling and leaving stupid messages about who loves who, ha ha. It was sickening. And as my mother got more involved with Encore Singles, the phone rang even oftener. My mother's voice was cool and businesslike when she answered.

I could hear Allison screaming, "Hello, this is Allison Poindexter, who's this?" and I went on contemplating the mess around my feet.

A few minutes later Allison came thundering up the stairs. She was only ten, but she was built like a small tank, with a thick, square body and big feet. My mother was scared to death she'd be tall like me, and then there would be two Amazons loose in the house. She ran awkwardly and heavily, and I called her Allison Elephant, which she hated. I don't blame her, but she got red in the face and absolutely enraged, and it seemed justice for the things she did to me. My mother said we are sisters and should be kind to each other, because Family Is Important. Charlotte said siblings are rarely kind to each other. She remembers how she fought with my father, even though she secretly idolized him. I don't think Allison idolizes me, even secretly. No reason she should.

"Phone call for *you*," she yelled two feet from my ear. "But first it was for me. It's Daddy." She thundered down the stairs ahead of me and parked herself right by the kitchen phone. She put her elbows on her knees and her chin in her hands with her fingers pulling down her cheeks to make grotesque faces.

I said hello in my most casual voice. This was only about the tenth time my father had called us since he left nine months before: on our birthdays, and at Thanksgiving, Christmas, Valentine's Day, and a few times in between. I was trying to think what holiday this might be. "Call me anytime, sweetie," he had told me the first time we talked after he left, but when I tried it once a woman answered and said he wasn't home but she would be glad to take a message.

"Hi, sweetie, how are you?" His voice made me think of strong black coffee and rough wool plaid shirts.

"Fine. I'm fine. How are *you?*" I am not a good conversationalist on the telephone. Or even off the telephone. Only in my head do I make brilliant, witty remarks that absolutely dazzle the people I imagine myself making them to. But that never happens in real life.

"Terrific. I'm wondering how you and Allison would like to come here to my place for dinner on Sunday?"

"This Sunday?" I asked. Even though he rarely called and even though we'd never seen where he lived, because he usually took us out for hamburgers unless it was a birthday and we went to The Steak Joint, even so, I should have sounded a little better than that.

"Yes. I'll pick you up about three. If it's a nice day, we can go ice skating, and if it's not a nice day we'll think up something else to do."

"Okay."

He asked about school and so on, and I answered with a brilliant range of single syllables, and then we hung up.

Allison started jumping up and down and yowling because she wanted to talk to him some more.

"You had your chance."

The dishes were rattling in the kitchen cupboards from the jumping. My mother came in from her bedroom. "What was *that* all about?"

Allison was still jumping, crash-crash, and shrieking, "We're going skating with Daddy and then to *his* house for dinner."

"Sunday," I added.

"Terrific," said my mother in a heavy voice. "Tell him—" and stopped. "Tell him to please get in touch with me."

The next morning it was partly raining, partly snowing. I tramped over to Laura's and belted down some lukewarm chocolate that she had saved for me. On the way to school, hunched over against the weather, I mentioned Dad's phone call and the plans for Sunday.

"How *is* Jack, anyway?" Laura did not believe in what she called "honorifics," like "Mister." Since most adults, except for Charlotte, do believe in titles and probably would like more of them, Laura had a reputation for being a smart-mouth. It's just that she thought titles were a sign of inequality.

"Okay, I guess."

"How long since you've heard from him?"

I knew she was looking for material for the ledger. According to the Poindexter entry, my father has unspecified visitation rights. Which he rarely exercises.

"A month, about," I mumbled. "I don't really keep track." It would be exactly thirty-seven days on Sunday.

"It's his problem, you know," Laura said. "Not yours.

It has nothing to do with you. He's feeling very guilty, is all. Just can't face his own feelings."

"Uh-huh." It was easy for me, I thought, even though he had been my best friend. But what about Allison? She didn't understand what I did. Allison was another problem on which Laura was working.

"Anyway, it should be quite interesting."

Sunday morning I woke up late, and I just could not bring myself to get out of bed. Somehow the sight of my room was more than I could bear. Before I even went out to the bathroom I started to shove the mess out of sight, into the closet, under the bed, anywhere. I was thinking, "My whole life is like this room," and I made a firm resolution to turn over a new leaf, clean it up, get organized, begin a brand new existence.

One of my biggest problems was that I couldn't stand to part with things. Practically everything I have ever owned was right there in my room, except for the stuff my mother sometimes came in and gathered up when I was not at home. Whole drawers and boxes of things disappeared that way, and sometimes I didn't notice until weeks or even months later. I got mad, but she said I would be buried alive if she didn't sometimes take drastic action.

Even so, my closet was stuffed with clothes. Most of them didn't fit me, and most of the rest I wouldn't wear for one reason or another. Charlotte always said clothes are costumes that make statements to other people about how we feel about ourselves. It's important, she said, to decide what kind of statement you want to make and then not be influenced by friends or trends. It's okay to change, but the change must come from within yourself. Charlotte always wears black, with different belts and scarves and jewelry. Her statement is very dramatic.

My statement was jeans, and I was hoping that I would never have to wear anything but jeans. Laura and I had made a solemn pact that we would never wear stockings, even when we have fabulous careers and are prominent in our respective fields. Since I did not yet have in mind a field in which I could be prominent, I wasn't concerned about what I would wear to work.

I was not even worried about not knowing what I was going to do with my life. Everyone else seemed to be. My aunt said there was plenty of time, and in the meanwhile I should be open to new experiences, which was her way of saying I better start thinking about it. Laura, who had known for years what she wanted to do, kept coming up with proposals, like being a gypsy fortune-teller. She thought my unusual height would make me more believable.

My mother worried from a different angle: when somebody mentioned college, she went into a tailspin and started yelling at me to study harder and improve my grades and to start cramming on vocabulary for the SATs; from there she started complaining about how my father did not give her enough child support money to keep us in shoes, much less to send us to college.

My father said not to worry, that I would only wind up getting married anyway, and all the money spent on education would really be just an investment in getting a husband for me who is capable of earning a living.

My mother snorted at this. "What happens if that husband in which you have invested leaves you in the lurch?"

My father suggested that I take typing and shorthand

and a secretarial course as "insurance." This was one thing my mother agreed with my father about. But Laura and Charlotte had heart attacks when I told them. "They'd never give that advice to a son," they both said.

Charlotte suggested that I take a year off to travel and see the world. If she had it to do over again, she'd hitch-hike around the country. She said I'd probably get a better education doing that than I would sitting in a college class-room. Then I could get whatever vocational training I needed to make a living—but not secretarial. Hitchhiking was not an idea that appealed to me. Maybe I have no sense of adventure.

What I was thinking about more and more, although I had not told anyone except Laura (and that was a mis-take), was going to live at Wisdom Peak after I graduated. That idea was implanted in my brain the night of Char-lotte's rap group, and I hadn't been able to let go of it. I got my aunt to give me her copies of *Pearls of Wisdom*, the newsletter Michael sent her, and I had read so much about it that I felt as though I had already been there. I made up my mind that when Charlotte and I went down there over spring vacation, I would put my name on the waiting list, if there was such a thing, just to be sure of getting in as soon as I had finished high school in two years.

I had thought and thought about how it would be when I'd be living there. There are dormitories where you can share a room or live by yourself, whichever you want. I thought it would be interesting to have a roommate, which I never had except for short periods when Allison and I were forced to stay in the same room together. Every-one eats in a common dining room, which according to

Pearls is like one big family and not at all like a school cafeteria. Everybody takes turns cooking, and the food is good because everybody cooks their favorites.

Wisdom Peak is not like other communes, because it was founded on sound organizational principles developed by a famous behavioral psychologist. Most communes are just a bunch of people who get together for a while, and they then find out how complicated it is to make a community work, and they start to drift away and the whole thing eventually collapses. But Wisdom Peak was started years ago, and it's still growing. They have a farm, with animals and orchards and fields and gardens. There are cows to milk and they've got a herd of sheep and some goats. Michael told Charlotte in a letter that one of the little goats follows him all around the place, like a pet. He calls him Ajax.

They have a business of making folk toys, and my intention was to work in the toy shop, if they'd teach me woodworking. I also had a few specialties for when it came my turn to cook, and I thought I'd enjoy working in the garden, although I never did that at home. Maybe there'd be a little goat to follow me around, too. I read that they swim in the river in the summer, and in the evening everybody who wants to gathers in the common room with instruments to play and sing, and sometimes there are dances. Once in a while they all climb in the old school bus and go into town to a movie. Michael said you have to work hard, but that you don't have to do anything you don't really want to do. The labor credit system is for making sure everybody does a fair share. He said it really is Utopia.

When I told Laura my plans, she said she'd give me from three to six months at Wisdom Peak or any other commune, Utopia or not. She said I was too much of an individualist, and that there was more to life than making toys or milking cows. It was her opinion (her semi-professional opinion, as she called it) that communes were for spineless creatures who lacked the ambition to make it in the real world. She thought Michael was probably a spineless creature.

"A commune is nothing more than a crowded womb," she said, in an authoritative tone of voice. "Some people need a womb-like existence in order to survive. You're not one of them. In fact, the sooner you get away from the womb you're in now, the better off you'll be. And I can't see you making toys for a career."

"I wasn't really thinking of it as a career. More as a stage to go through."

"The one thing I do approve of is that attitude toward children," Laura admitted. "It's very healthful. Furthermore, you know, the parents don't raise the children. The community does. You don't have to pay a bit of attention to your kid, unless you want to. The kids live in their own separate house, and they're taken care of by people who have the proper knack for taking care of them."

"How do you know all this?"

"Wisdom Peak didn't invent the idea. B. F. Skinner did. I've read some of his books. A psychologist. Considering how most parents mess up their kids, it's probably a good idea."

"How do you know the community won't mess up the kid?"

"No guarantee, of course. But it's less of an ego trip for someone other than the child's biological parents."

I thought it was a crummy idea, but beyond saying

53

that I had no intellectual arguments. Just feelings. Laura had read all the books, and I didn't know who Skinner was.

Probably in my case, though, if I ever do have children, which seems unlikely because I don't think I will ever marry, it would be better to have them raised by a community. I don't think I would be much good around children. I'm certainly not much good with Allison. My mother used to try to get me babysitting jobs with her friends, but I always refused.

The idea was to get me to earn my own spending money. My mother said that when she was my age she had a job cleaning her dentist's office on weekends. I wouldn't last two days, she said, because I have an inability to see dirt right under my nose. My mother is a very good housekeeper, and I imagine the dentist had a spotlessly clean office. I hoped they wouldn't want me to do much cleaning at Wisdom Peak. Certainly they'd never send me to take care of the children.

Any time Laura wanted a part-time job she could get one as a sales clerk in a boutique owned by one of her parents' clients. But Laura claimed she had more important things to do with her time than to stand around watching people trying to make up their minds which useless item to buy. Her parents had set up a checking account for her with enough money to cover all her expenses for a year. That was to teach her to budget, but she didn't need to be taught. She always had money left over. She has offered to manage my financial affairs, which I promised to let her do as soon as I have any financial affairs to manage.

I couldn't even manage my own clothes. By two o'clock Sunday afternoon, with my father due in an hour, I had separated them into piles of dresses, shirts, skirts, and pants. Then I had subdivided these into piles of things that fit and things that didn't fit. But most things that fit I didn't like, and some things that didn't fit I was very fond of. I frequently disliked things that were otherwise fine because of something that happened to me when I was wearing them.

For instance, there was a light green dress with a big white collar. One day, about a year before my father left, we were at the hardware store together, and on the way home we passed a shop with this dress in the window. He said, "I bet you'd look good in that. Why don't you go in and try it on?" I didn't want to but he talked me into it. It fit perfectly and he bought it for me.

He had never done anything like that before. Even my mother was amazed. It was my all-time favorite special-occasion dress. I wore it the day I had to make the speech in assembly welcoming the seventh graders on behalf of the ninth graders, and then somehow I forgot all my lines, absolutely everything, and I just stood there on the stage, staring out at all those faces. Teachers hissed at me from the wings, trying to get me to say something. Finally I yelled, "WELCOME," and ran off the stage. After that every time I looked at the green dress I thought of the disaster, and I couldn't stand to wear it again. Charlotte said I should bury it for a week or something to exorcise the evil spirits.

I also came across the beautiful blouse Charlotte brought me from Mexico with birds and flowers embroidered across the front and down the sleeves. I used to wear it constantly, when Jimmy Schwartz hung around my locker a lot. Jimmy had practically memorized *The Guinness Book of World Records*, and he knew things like the world's biggest sausage was made in Germany in 1601, was three thousand feet long, and was carried through the streets by 103 butchers. And he always managed to get the statistics into his conversation very cleverly—when we had hot dogs for lunch, for instance. Jimmy was hoping that I would eventually be tall enough to be included in *The Guinness Book.* Jimmy said the tallest woman alive at the time the book was published was eight feet two inches tall. I would have to grow only a little more than two feet to match her. Then Jimmy's father was transferred and he took his book of records and moved to Cincinnati. I missed him, even though he had been a pest sometimes. He was the only person who saw my height as an advantage. The blouse was now too tight across the shoulders, but I couldn't part with it because it reminded me of him.

I found the dress my mother made for me to go visit my grandfather the last time before he died, and my lucky sweater for getting good marks on tests, and a shirt that somebody once said made me look sexy but had gotten unsexy green paint stains on the front of it.

I was not making much progress. I started resorting things, throwing stuff I absolutely had to get rid of into a pile in one corner to take to Goodwill. Then I remembered the articles I had read in *Pearls* about "community clothing" at Wisdom Peak. You don't own your clothes there. Instead there's a big attic lined with racks and boxes full of clothes, all kinds of stuff, and you can go and take whatever you want to wear. You can dress up in a fencing costume, or wear a fireman's hat, if you feel like it, although mostly everybody wears jeans and the girls sometimes put on long skirts. The one style they have, sort of a trademark, is that you never wear socks that match. It started out because it was a pain to sort the socks, and there always seemed to be some odd ones left over when the laundry crew sent the clean stuff back up to the attic. So everybody started to wear whatever socks they grabbed.

So I got this bright idea: I'd pack all my clothes up and take them with me when I moved to Wisdom Peak, and I'd turn them all over to community clothing. I hoped there would be some other tall girls there, so I wouldn't always end up wearing my own clothes anyway.

Since I didn't have any boxes handy right then, I decided just to leave everything where it was until I could get some at the liquor store. Just then my mother came in to find out why she hadn't seen me all day. And she took one look at the clothes that were all over the place—she didn't notice that they were really sorted in piles—and started to have a fit, bawling me out for being messy and not taking care of my clothes, and so on. She was standing there in an old pair of knitted slacks gone baggy at the knees and seat and a man's plaid shirt, and she was yelling, "I just don't see how anyone can live in a mess like this!" I started to tell her that I was reviewing my whole life and planning my future. But instead I shoved all the clothes back in my closet again and slammed the door on them.

Then I heard Allison screeching, "Daddy's here, come on, jerk, he's *here*."

I dived into the closet again and grabbed the Mexican shirt, whch lay on top of a pile, and rooted around until I located a skirt. I stuck my feet into some clogs and got upset because I couldn't find my jacket before I figured out that it was somewhere downstairs and not in this mess at all.

Allison and Dad were yakking away in the car. I

57

climbed in shivering, because it had turned colder again and my legs were completely bare. Allison had brushed and combed her hair herself and tied bows of yarn in it, and she looked very pretty. That made me feel worse. I had forgotten to fix my hair back, the way my father liked it. I had been letting it grow long, and he liked me to pull it into a kind of twist that he said made me look quite mature and sophisticated. But it was just hanging down loose and straight, exactly the way he didn't like it.

"Hello, beautiful," said my father, as though he didn't even notice my hair. I liked that, even though I knew he was lying.

Because of the weather, we were going bowling instead of skating. I don't much like to bowl, and Allison didn't know how, and Dad always used to say it was a dumb game that gave you muscles in only one arm. It didn't turn out well. First we had to wait a long time to get a lane, and then Allison couldn't find a ball that was light enough, and I had my usual problem getting shoes big enough. "Your ma must be feeding you some fancy vitamins," observed the old codger behind the counter, slapping down a pair of musty-smelling men's shoes for me.

Allison rolled her balls so slowly that they practically stopped before they dribbled off into the gutter, and she was getting all upset and frustrated. Then one of them kept on going, you could see it turning over and over, the same orange dot coming up, and it eased against the pins which all quietly fell down as though they had fainted. It was a strike, and Allison shrieked and gloated and carried on until I wanted to smack her.

I got no strikes, one spare, and a few gutter balls. My score was 75, and I split open the Mexican blouse under both arms. Dad, who is very well coordinated, got 185 in a game he doesn't even like. Allison did not score any more points, none at all, and her face got red but instead of crying she started pestering for candy bars and potato chips.

Dad was firm. "You'll spoil your dinner."

So Allison teased me about my torn blouse and how she could see *everything* through the split seam.

Finally we left the alleys. The cold rain had stopped, and there was a little thin sunshine. I was shivering again in my short skirt. "Spring's just around the corner," Dad observed merrily.

Allison insisted on sitting in the front seat of his little car again, and I had to crawl in back where there was hardly any room at all for my long legs. I started to protest but stopped immediately. No sense in spoiling the day for him by complaining. It turned out to be a long drive to his place. He wouldn't tell us anything about it; he just kept saying, "You'll see." Allison had referred to it as a house, but I decided it must be an apartment in one of the big new condominiums that were being advertised: "Number One Strawberry Hill is Stanhope's Number One Address." He'd want something classy, like Les Artistes where Moozy lived.

But we drove right past the area where the apartments were, and through the residential section and wound up on a strip of garages and diners and hardware stores. Finally about the time my legs lost all feeling from being doubled up under my chin, he turned down a narrow driveway between Rich Motors and Solomon Brothers Bakery to a cement block building with FULLERTON CARPETS FACTORY-TO-YOU WAREHOUSE painted along one entire side in red letters. He parked his Volkswagen among the Used Car

Specials with big Rich Motors sales tags on the windshields. We climbed out, wondering what was going on, and followed him to a little door that you hardly noticed next to the Fullerton Carpets loading platform. He unlocked the door and motioned us in. Then he locked and double-locked the door behind us. The stairway was narrow, steep, and dark, and there was a plain wooden door at the top of it. Allison hung back, and so did I. But he urged us on, up the steep, dark stairs. The door at the top was opened by a smiling woman wearing a red and white checked apron. The first thing I saw after her smile was her fat ankles and heavy calves. There was a smell of cooking behind her.

"Hello, everybody," she said cheerfully, looking at each of us but mostly at Dad.

Allison and I mumbled Hi and Dad said, "Hello, beautiful," and when he got to the top of the stairs he hugged her and put a big kiss on her cheek, winking at me while he did. I wondered if she knew that he calls me beautiful, too. I felt sour enough to tell her. The top part of her was thin. He had not hugged me in months. Dad made introductions. The name of the woman in the apron was Elizabeth, but she wanted us to call her Libby, "as all my friends do." She already knew our names and she shook hands with us.

The room was big and bright and not at all what you would expect to find over a carpet warehouse. I recognized the yellow canvas chairs that used to be on our porch and a rickety old card table from the playroom. Near the window sat a beat-up metal office desk and a typist's chair patched with black tape. There were no rugs or curtains but there were drawings and photographs tacked to the wall and a few rangy philodendron reaching toward the window. Some kitchen equipment was along one wall and a huge bed against the opposite wall.

Allison discovered that it was a water bed. My father saw her sitting bug-eyed on the edge of it and laughed. "Want to try it?"

I sat down on it carefully, but Allison took a flying leap and we sloshed back and forth on it for a while. "After I get a couch you two can come for the night and sleep on the water bed. How's that sound, Allie Baby?"

"Does that mean C.C.'s going to sleep with me, too?" Allie Baby wanted to know. Any time we've had to sleep in the same bed it has been a night-long battle for territory.

"We'll worry about that when the time comes," Dad said, to avert a major crisis. "Now what can I get you gals to drink?"

Apparently we were going to have cocktails, an adult custom I find incredibly boring. I don't like to sip soft drinks in short glasses with ice cubes and maraschino cherries, but Allison does.

"Orange soda," said my sister.

"Grape, please."

Dad consulted with Libby and reported, "We're fresh out of orange and grape. How about gingerale? Or one Coke to split?"

Allison got the Coke. Libby was arranging a tray with snacks and dips. Dad struggled with the ice cubes. He mixed two drinks for himself and Libby and two make-believe cocktails for us. He put the glasses on the tray which was set on a wicker basket in the middle of the floor between the porch chairs. Everything got passed around, and Allison had already gulped down half her Coke when

61

Dad held up his glass to propose a toast: "To my women-folk." He nodded at each of us, and Libby said, "Hear, hear," which made him chuckle.

We all drank. I took a good look at him. I thought he had gained weight, and something else was different. Maybe his mustache? There seemed to be more of it. And his hair was longer.

"Libby is a writer," my father announced, reaching over to pat her arm. "She writes children's books. Isn't that terrific?" He beamed at her and patted her again, this time on the behind when she got up to reach for the carrot sticks. I tried to remember if he ever patted my mother on the behind and couldn't think of a single time. Libby grinned at him and sat down in a hurry. She did not look like my idea of an author, especially of children's books. I had always pictured them as wispy old ladies who own a lot of cats and drink a lot of tea with milk. There was nothing wispy about Libby.

"Story books?" Allison wanted to know. "Fairy tales and junk like that?"

"No, not story books," Libby answered, and then my father took over as her spokesman. "Books about, uh, real things, like how cheese is made and how the farmer gets his eggs to market. Really interesting books. I'm going to get some for you."

"I only like story books about real people," Allison informed them flatly. "No animals. No bears or spiders."

"She hated Winnie the Pooh," I contributed.

"Next time I'll bring you one of my books," Libby offered in a friendly tone, "and you can see for yourself."

"How many books have you written?" I asked Libby, because I had the feeling that Allison was going to make some more embarrassing remarks.

"Eight," she said. "Six already published, one in production and coming out next fall, and one that I'm just finishing up. But I have contracts for two more when I finish this one, and then I have a few more simmering somewhere in the back of my brain."

"This gal is so full of ideas it scares me," my father said, and he blew her a kiss and winked. She grinned again.

Allison had polished off a bowl of nuts almost single-handedly and was looking around for something else to munch besides carrots and celery.

"You must be hungry," Libby said, watching her. "I'd better get things going."

"Libby has cooked up something very special for you," said my father. "I told her you like spicy things."

"I *hate* spicy things," said Allison, sounding hurt.

"You do?"

We both do. He had forgotten. How could he forget a thing like that?

"Maybe you'll like this," Libby said. "It's a curry, and I made it very mild, just in case."

"What's curry?" Allison was already wrinkling her nose.

"Well, it's a blend of different kinds of exotic spices— turmeric, I think, and cardomom and cumin and I forget what else. There are different ways of blending it. And then you use it to flavor meat or fish or rice."

"I don't like it," Allison said. "Haven't you got anything else to eat?" She whimpered, as though she was going to starve to death on the spot.

"Try it anyway, princess," Dad coaxed. "Libby wrote a book called *Spices Around the World*, so she knows all about these things. I'll bet it's in your school library."

"The English invented curries," Libby explained from

the stove, sounding like a fifth grade geography teacher, "and took them to India during the Colonial period. They used them the way spices were all originally used, to disguise the taste of rotting meat."

"Is this meat rotten we're supposed to eat?"

"Goodness, Allison, I hope not!"

I was embarrassed for Allison, who was acting even dumber than usual. I should have felt sorry for Libby, because she seemed to be trying hard to please us, except I knew it wasn't really us she was trying to please. It was Dad.

"Here, love, let me help you," offered my father, and he started to carry things the three steps from the stove to the card table, which had been set with four places. We dragged our porch chairs up to the table, and Dad wheeled the desk chair over for Allison, because the others were too low. He spun it to make it high enough for her. There was hardly any room under the table for my long legs and Dad's.

Libby set down a big bowl of rice and another big bowl of shrimp swimming in a greenish-yellow sauce, among several small bowls of things I didn't recognize. She continued to instruct us about curries and condiments. "That bright orange stuff is chutney," and then she told us how chutney is made, with mangoes and so on.

"Yuk," said Allison, staring unhappily at all the bowls. Finally she scooped a big pile of rice onto her plate. "Where's the butter?"

"In the fridge. I'll get it," Libby volunteered.

"She can get it herself," said Dad, beginning to sound annoyed.

Allison spun around on the desk chair, got the butter, put a big wad of it on top of the rice, and carefully buried it. Then she slowly sipped her milk. When she tested with her fork a minute later, the wad of butter was still there. "The butter isn't melting," she complained. "The rice isn't hot enough."

"Shall I put it in a pan and heat it up for you? Maybe you want to try a little curried shrimp on it before I do."

"I hate shrimp. I hate that yellow glop. I hate this whole meal."

"Allison, just shut up and eat," my father ordered, out of patience. Allison started to bawl.

"Don't force her, Jack," Libby said.

"Damned if she's going to sit here and talk like that," barked my father, and he slapped the card table with the palm of his hand, making the dishes clatter and all of us jump and Allison wail like a banshee. "Leave the table, Allison."

Allison, blubbering, rushed off to flop on the water bed and snuffle loudly for her irritated audience. Meanwhile I was eating the curry and the chutney and other condiments and finding out that it wasn't bad after all. My father and Libby looked at me with such gratitude that I took a huge second helping of everything. I didn't like it all *that* much, but somebody had to do something, and eating is one of my major talents. Maybe my only one. After a while Allison snuffled wetly one more time and climbed back on the secretarial chair. She proceeded to devour every speck of the rice, which was really cold by then. Next she discovered that if you spin one way on the chair it gets higher, and if you spin the other way it gets lower. She spun and spun, making us all dizzy. Finally Dad grabbed her. "That's enough," he said. And she sat there looking completely cockeyed.

Dad remembered that this was supposed to be a party,

65

and he was the host. "So now you've had an authentic Indian dinner," he said. "It was a triumph, Libby, a culinary masterpiece." He got up and walked around the card table and kissed her and started rubbing her shoulders, at which point I got up too and started carrying piles of dishes over to the tiny sink. But I couldn't find any place to stack them.

"Sit down, honey, you're a guest today."

I was not going to watch them. "Guests always help," I told him. "Come on, Allison, you can help too."

"Where's the dishwasher?" she asked, pouting.

"We're it. I'll wash, and you can dry."

She sighed. "Next time, Daddy, I want to go *out* to eat, like we used to."

"Next time, Allie," he said, "you can eat at home."

She began to bawl again. Dad started to get red in the face, but Libby reached over and touched his arm. "She'll be all right, darling. Give her time."

Libby organized the cleaning up, and we all got in each others' way, especially Allison, but finally it was done. Then Libby pulled out a Parcheesi board and set it up on the card table. She explained that it was originally an Indian game, and Dad put in that Libby was now working on a book about games around the world. Allison perked up at that one: she loves games. I hate them. But we played on and on, because at last we had found something that Allison liked to do. She cheated very cleverly, but it wasn't necessary; we all wanted her to win, because we couldn't face any more of her tantrums. At last it was time to go home.

"Next time we get together," my father said, buttoning Allison into her coat as though she were a baby, "maybe

Libby will bring her children."

Libby's children? I hadn't thought of that. "I have two sons and a daughter," she told us. "Scott is fourteen, Billy is twelve, and Jennifer is just your age, Allison. They're with their father this weekend."

We had been so busy with the food and the information about spices and India and Indian food and the endless game of Parcheesi that I had not really thought very much about Libby, except that my father liked her. Allison must have been tired. She just looked a little dazed and nodded her head and snuggled up against Dad. "Let's go."

Dad nudged us and we said thank you and good night to Libby, who seemed to be staying later, and then we started home. "Enjoy yourselves?" Dad asked on the way.

I told him yes, and Allison said sort of.

"Libby is a fine person," Dad informed us. "I think you'll become very fond of her. At least, I hope so."

When we got out of the car, I remembered Mom's message. "Mother wants you to get in touch with her."

"She knows where I am," he snapped. Then he hugged us and said, "Be good kids." He waited until we were on the porch before he started to back down the drive.

"He didn't even say 'See you soon,'" Allison growled sleepily.

Mom was sitting in the kitchen, drinking tea. "How was your day?"

"Good," I said, figuring that was enough, but suddenly Allison was awake and giving her a detailed description of the bowling and the Parcheesi and everything that happened in between.

"Who is Libby?" my mother finally got a chance to ask.

"Daddy's girl friend," said Allison, annoyed at a question with such an obvious answer. Then she told Mom about Libby being a writer who writes children's books, a real author of lots and lots of books, tons of them, and how the library probably had them and when could they go and get some? Allison always did have a remarkable sense of timing.

"What's she like, Allison?"

Allison squinted to remember exactly. "Old," she said. "Almost as old as you. She doesn't have any gray hair, but that's because she dyes it. She's sort of fat below and skinny up top. She wears contact lenses."

How did she know all that? In between tantrums, Allison was a very good observer.

"She calls him 'Jack Darling.'" Allison imitated Libby extravagantly, "'Jack Darling, would you pass the chutney?'"

Sometimes my sister Allison is really quite funny.

Chapter Four

Allison rumbled up the stairs to wake me, over-joyed that I had overslept and provided her with this opportunity. She does not simply knock on the door and say, "Time to get up, C.C." No, she bangs with both fists, screeching and hollering. Until I put a small lock on my door she used to bang on *me* with both fists. My mother does not approve of locks on doors, but Allison is not her sister.

It was very late. I jumped up and grabbed the Mexican shirt with the rips under the arms and the wrinkled denim skirt that were lying on the floor next to my bed, dragged a comb through my hair, and rushed downstairs. No time to wash or even to brush teeth. My mother, wearing a raspberry-colored bathrobe with a drooping satin bow at the collar and purplish rings under her eyes, took one quick look and said, "Go back and start over."

I began to argue, decided arguing was a waste of time, and went. But I refused breakfast, even though I was hungry as always. "French test first period," I mumbled, shooting out the door. There wasn't time to go to Laura's, but we had a standing agreement that if I was not there by 7:35 she went without me. It was drizzling, my raincoat was in my locker at school, and by the time I raced across Kings Highway I was drenched. But I made it on time: I slid into my seat just as the bell rang.

Mrs. Carpenter, the French teacher, was not there. At her desk sat Mr. McDermott, the gypsy-eyed poet, which meant that Laura would be showing up soon, even though she was not taking French. For a wildly optimistic moment I hoped we'd write poetry instead of taking the test. But Mrs. Carpenter had left the dittoed sheets for us, and after they were passed out our substitute with one finger joint missing disappeared behind a book. We could hear him snickering to himself, probably at something raunchy. The test was hard and I was wet and tired and had not studied the right vocabulary lists. When the bell rang I left for history. Sue Brodie, who considers herself maturely attractive and also had history at the other end of the building, was propped on her elbows in front of Mr. McDermott, her big breasts right under his nose, her rear end sticking out. For some reason that made me mad, but I resisted the temptation to give her a good smack just on general principles.

At lunch time I met Laura in the cafeteria. Spicy Sloppy Joes on Toasty Buns, Creamy Cole Slaw, Rich Chocolate Cake. In spite of it she seemed depressed, and I figured it was something to do with McDermott. She told me her parents had come back from their trips, but other than that news she didn't have much to say. She barely mentioned McDermott and she forgot to ask me about

Sunday dinner at my father's, which was okay since I didn't much feel like talking about it then anyway. She said she had madrigal group rehearsal after school, so I decided to stop by and see my aunt before I walked home alone.

Charlotte was in her little office in one corner of the art room, her face wrinkled with concern for somebody in the chair next to her desk. The somebody was Jeannie Chelminski, our head cheerleader, who I recognized by the long red hair that hangs around her shoulders like a silk curtain. While I waited for Jeannie to come out, I wandered around the art room, which was jammed with all kinds of weird-looking projects. Del D'Ottavia was working on her Bunny Bed, a big wooden contraption that somewhat resembled a rabbit you could lie down on. There were two big pink lightbulbs for eyes and a rubber ball with a squeaker inside for a nose. Del had glued pink velvet padding inside the tall pointy ears. Del told everybody it was functional sculpture, but it looked silly and uncomfortable and it was the kind of project that sometimes got Charlotte in trouble with a parents' group that was always snooping around the school and then writing letters to the *Greenfield Sentinel* about how their tax dollars were being wasted and their children corrupted. The art department, meaning my aunt, has been mentioned four times in letters to "Voice of the People" on the editorial page, and she has been named by name on two other occasions. She wrote back, "Process is more important than product at this stage of individual development. It's my task to assist in the process, not to determine the product."

Jeannie Chelminski rushed out of Charlotte's office, her beautiful hair floating in ripples around her nicely freckled face. Her green eyes were swollen and her face

71

was blotchy from crying. Jeannie is on the swim team, gets good grades, has lots of friends of both sexes; so why was she running out of the art teacher's office looking like total misery?

"Advice to the lovelorn, free," Charlotte called out to me when Jeannie had gone.

I flopped in the visitor's chair that Jeannie had been in and stretched my legs halfway across the tiny office. "What's her problem?"

"McDermott."

"Her too? I thought she stuck to football heroes and class presidents."

"They're boys," she said. "McDermott is a man."

"Oh."

"How come you seem to be immune to the McDermott magic?"

I twirled my thumbs frontward and then backward and passed on the first thing that came into my head. "I don't know. Maybe because I'm taller than he is."

"What an incredibly stupid reason!" she yelped. "A stupid, sexist reason!"

Then the lecture began—the whole idea that the man has to be taller, smarter, and older, and generally superior in every way, except morals, is based on sexism. It shouldn't matter which is which, Charlotte preached; a man who is sure of himself is not threatened by a woman who may happen to be taller or smarter or older or even stronger, and a truly liberated woman wouldn't give a second thought to any such differences. *Et cetera*. I'd heard it all before. "It's all a matter of mutual respect," she said.

Naturally she was right. She nearly always was. She believes she is liberal and open-minded, which she is. But it was impossible to argue with her. If I hadn't been so tired I would never have said the wrong thing in the first place. The main reason I did not have a crush on Mr. McDermott was, one, I don't really like poetry that much, even though I put it on my list of things I like to do most for Moozy's rap group, and, two, I think he's full of babalooey.

Charlotte finally ran out of lectures and invited me to her house for supper. "Let's see—tomorrow is my yoga class, Wednesday is rap group, Thursday I have pottery, Friday I'm going out. What about tonight?"

"Okay." I didn't think I could wait even four more hours to ask her about Michael and Wisdom Peak, and I thought of saying something right then. But I could see she was looking at something behind me, out in the art room, and she wasn't quite paying attention any more.

"I'll see you later then," she said. "Come about five thirty. I'll drive you home afterwards so you won't have to ride your bike in the dark."

When I got up to leave I saw Mr. McDermott stretched out on the Bunny Bed, pretending to be sound asleep.

And I practically fell over Laura, who was hovering in the shadows outside the art room, gazing at McDermott on the Bunny Bed. "I thought you had madrigal practice," I said.

"I cut." She wouldn't look me in the eye.

We walked home in almost total silence. I started to tell her about Dad and Libby and hear what she thought of the new development in the Poindexter Situation, but I hadn't even gotten to the main part of my story when I realized she wasn't listening. It just was not my day to

73

command attention.

"You aren't listening," I accused her.

"Yes I am."

"You're not. Tell me what I just said."

She shrugged. Laura, who was not a moody person and never had much patience with people who were, might as well have been on another planet. I figured it was McDermott who had her in an uproar, and that she'd tell me what was on her mind when she felt like it. We walked the rest of the way to my house without speaking.

My mother, with yellow rollers nested in her hair like plastic canaries, was sliding chocolate chip cookies off a blackened baking sheet and onto a wire rack already crowded with lots more chocolate chip cookies. Somebody must be coming, I thought; who was it this time? She greeted us with her usual, "What's new in the world of education?"

Laura said, "Nothing," and left without taking a cookie or even getting a good whiff of the tomato sauce simmering on the stove.

"What's wrong with *her?*"

"Don't know." I snitched three cookies, trying to make it look as though I was taking only one.

"The Fact Finders are meeting here tonight," she said. "Try to leave a few for them."

My mother was chairperson of a committee to figure out why there was only one man for every four point seven women in Encore Singles. When they knew that, they hoped to figure out how to change it to a better ratio. They decided to meet at our house twice a month—five women, including Mrs. Panek, and a Mr. Kruger who stammers. When Mr. Kruger wasn't there, the five women agreed that he was not exactly the kind of man they wanted to attract to the group, even to improve the ratio. There were already too many Mr. Krugers in Encore Singles.

I wasn't anxious to tell my mother about Charlotte's invitation for supper. I expected her not to be too happy, because of her general attitude toward Charlotte, but she had her way of getting even. "Too bad," she said when I finally mentioned it. "There's a pan of lasagne in the oven." Which was my all-time-never-to-be-equaled favorite, and we both knew Charlotte would probably be serving some kind of soybeans.

While Allison and I were arguing about who was supposed to clean up afterwards, since it was my night and I wasn't going to be there, Mrs. Panek came by to help my mother get ready for the Fact Finders. Mrs. Panek was dressed in jeans very tight in the seat and her hair was tied in two little pigtails with red yarn that matched her tight sweater. She looked like an extremely fatigued sixteen-year-old. While my mother set out coffee cups and spoons, Mrs. Panek talked. "We *know* the problem. The problem is younger women. Men in their forties want to date girls in their twenties, maybe even girls C.C.'s age, for God's sake. But a forty-five-year-old woman, even if she keeps her figure and her skin, attracts only those few rare men who have gotten past their adolescent ego trips. Men who are mature enough to recognize the value of a meaningful relationship with another mature person." Which I guessed must be Mrs. Panek, who works very hard to look like one of the younger women she doesn't approve of.

"What kind of an ego trip do you suppose Kruger is on?" my mother asked, and they both laughed.

Allison and I settled our argument: I agreed to wash

and dry all the dishes for the next two nights. Then I went upstairs to do my homework and escape from the giggling of the two Fact Finders, since Mrs. Panek was going to stay and eat my share of the lasagne. But I couldn't concentrate on my algebra, and I kept checking the clock until it was time to haul out my bike, a ten-speed reduced to operating in one gear thanks to Allison, and started pedaling.

It was only a fifteen-minute trip from our place to Charlotte's, but it was like going to a different world. In our part of town it was a big thing to have green grass so perfect that it looked artificial. Charlotte's neighborhood was practically a wilderness.

Her driveway was really just a rough gravel track. The house, which had once been a small stable, was almost completely hidden behind a grove of trees back off the road. Charlotte pulled open the rough plank door and Hugo, her Saint Bernard, shuffled out to greet me. Huge-O, as we sometimes called him, was beautiful and affectionate and totally stupid, the kind of dog who would offer to shake hands with a burglar. Hugo was so big he made Charlotte's place look like a large doghouse. I told Charlotte once that the house was just right for Snow White and the Seven Dwarfs. She laughed at that and said she was hardly Snow White, but if I knew any dwarfs who might qualify I should be sure to send them around.

Charlotte was tying a striped apron over her black pants and black sweater. "Have a look around and see what's new," she said. "I'll have this ready in a flash. Light some candles if you want to."

I found wicks in two formless waxy blobs on the table and used up a half-dozen matches lighting them. Long shadows leaped toward the high ceiling. A couple of mattresses were stacked next to one wall, covered with a furry rug and heaped with all kinds of pillows. That's where she slept. The table in front of it was an assemblage of driftwood and a slice of a strangely shaped tree with all kinds of whorls and knots in it. There were more squashy pillows on the floor around it to sit on while you ate.

There was always something new at Charlotte's. She made things and had them around for a while, and then she gave them to somebody or traded them and got something else, a present from another craftsperson or something she'd picked up at a sale. Paintings and drawings and collages hung on the walls and small pieces of sculpture sat on the mantle of the rough stone fireplace in the corner. Magazines and newspapers and books slumped in piles on the floor and on long boards propped on bricks. An easel and stacks of canvases leaned against the wall next to the enormous window that went all the way to the ceiling. The last daylight filtered through an avalanche of hanging plants and miniature stained glass pieces. The room was a gallery and a studio and a living place, full of coffee mugs and squeezed-out paint tubes and yarn and growing things in the kind of jumble I love.

I wandered into the room next to it, which was originally supposed to be the bedroom. When Michael and Jebby were with her, it was theirs, and she let them do whatever they wanted to with it, which was to tape magazine pictures of nude women all over the walls. That shocked my mother when she saw it; she thought twelve was much too young for frontal nudity. It bothered Charlotte, too, who saw it as a sign of developing male chauvinism.

77

After Jebby went away to stay with Uncle Ted and Michael took off for Wisdom Peak, Charlotte left their room the way it was for a while. When the boys didn't come home to visit she tore down all the nudes and packed up all their gear, books and games and baseball mitts and empty gerbil cages and so on. She painted the walls stark white and put white covers over the beds and tacked a white sheet on the floor. When she was finished it looked like a monk's cell, except for the candles and incense burner. She called it her Meditation Room, and she told me that she went there twice a day to sit on the floor in the Lotus Position.

But my aunt and I have a lot in common. First she propped a couple of blank canvases in one corner of the room—they were white, so you hardly noticed them—then more and more stuff followed for "temporary" storage. When I looked in, the Meditation Room was almost as cluttered as the studio, and it wasn't so white any more.

"Come here and see my new hanging," she called from the kitchen. "One of the kids in the Craft Club made it for me." An astrological chart, done in batik, was fastened above the sink. "It's my sign, Gemini," Charlotte explained, "and there's my moon, Virgo, and up there's my ascendant, Aquarius. It was an exchange deal. One of the kids is interested in astrology, too, so I worked out her chart—she's a typical Libra, very talented—and she did the hangings, one for herself and one for me. Aren't the colors fantastic?"

Charlotte considered it a challenge to teach in Greenfield High School, because Greenfield is schizophrenic—part of it WASP upper middle class with daddies who get on the train for New York every morning, part of it blue-collar with Italian and Hungarian names, and part of it poor blacks. Charlotte started an after-school crafts club, and some of the kids who had been punching holes in the walls and ripping out light fixtures started to come in and work on original projects.

"The colors are terrific," I agreed.

"Listen, there's some real talent around that school, if I could just get them to approve a bigger budget for the art department." Charlotte squinted into the broiler and flipped our soy-rice burgers. "Basketball, yes. Track, yes. Marching band, yes. Art, no. Want to carry in that salad?"

I rattled through the bead curtain in the doorway and put the salad—bean sprouts and some kind of seeds—on the table between the candles and went back to the kitchen for silverware, which she kept in a little basket hanging on the frame of the doorway. My mother would never put our silverware in an unusual place like that. My mother subscribes to *House Beautiful*, and she is really very clever about decorating. Our living room, for instance, is green and white with melon accents, and everyone who comes there says how lovely it is, which is true. But it is not a place you can ever be messy in, and I am by nature messy. I felt more at home at Charlotte's.

I had the idea of hanging bead curtains at the window of my room and putting blue bulbs in the ceiling light and calling it my "studio." I like the sound of that. When I was about twelve my parents fixed up my room with flowered wallpaper and French Provincial furniture and a ruffled canopy over the bed. It was supposed to make me more feminine. I liked it at first, but gradually I started to hate it. I wanted to paint over the flowers and give the bed to my sister and lay the mattress on the floor with piles of pillows on it. My mother put her foot down to all of that.

Charlotte came out with the soy-rice burgers off-centered on two white pottery plates and set them on the table. I tried to look pleased. "You know, I feel *so* much better since I've become a vegetarian," she said. "Ten times more energy and much less anger than when I was eating red meat."

"Don't you ever get hungry for a real hamburger?" I was dying for one, with lots of French fries and onion rings.

"Never," she said. "As a matter of fact, the thought of eating animal flesh turns my stomach." We bit into our food. Actually it wasn't terrible. But I kept thinking how good a hamburger would taste. "Listen," Charlotte said between mouthfuls, "did I tell you I'm thinking of changing my name?"

"But you just changed it back to Poindexter, didn't you? What do you want to change it to now?"

"No, this time my first name. Charlotte to Charlene."

"That sounds totally crazy! Why would you want to do a thing like that?"

She was sitting cross-legged on the floor, neat as a pretzel, and I was still trying to find a comfortable position. "I've been reading a book about numerology, and I'm convinced that we really are influenced by a lot of things, like the number of letters in our names, and so on. A friend of mine changed her name from Susan to Suzanne, and her life started improving the same week. The numbers just weren't right for her, with a name like Susan. Suzanne was perfect."

"But what if it turns out not to be for the better, but for the worse? Or if nothing happens? Can you change it again? Just keep changing your name until your luck improves?"

"Luck has nothing to do with it."

"Are there any more soy-rice burgers?"

We split the third one, and Charlotte/Charlene served wheat-germ-honey-carob pudding for dessert. Charlotte is anti-chocolate as well as anti-sugar. Philosophically I'm a vegetarian too, but I really am not crazy about the food.

"How about some tea?" She jumped up and put the kettle on and came back to let me sniff some different herb mixtures that all smelled like the dust you find under a bed. I picked one, and while we waited for it to brew she laid a small fire in the fireplace. My mother doesn't like to use our fireplace because she says it creates a lot of dirt.

She poured some of the tea into one smooth blue-glazed mug which she handed to me, and the rest into a lumpy orange-streaked cup with an uneven edge and no handle. She folded easily back down to the floor and cradled the cup in her palms.

"You know the story of this cup, don't you? Before my friend Peter left for New Mexico, he made two cups from the same ball of clay, pinch method, using his fingers. He gave one of them to me and took the other one. It was his way of keeping us in touch, even though we were apart."

"Peter the Potter pinched a pretty pair. . . ." I trailed off lamely, after my clever start. Typical.

"Yeah," she said glumly, staring into her lopsided cup. "Then he got married. How about that?"

Charlotte always seemed to have trouble with her men. Things would go well for a while, and then something seemed to happen.

She sprang up again and got very busy hooking up a wooden rod tied with rough brown string. Macramé knots had been worked for about six inches down from the rod, and the rest of the string had been wound up in clumps.

"It's a screen," she explained, "for the kitchen doorway. To replace the beads." She rattled a box of clay balls and cylinders. "A friend sent me these from Colorado. They'll be part of the design."

"What are you going to do with the bead curtain?"

"Give it to Goodwill, I guess."

"Could I have it?"

"Sure! Take it with you tonight, if you want."

"Terrific!" I'd just go ahead and hang it and not bother to mention it to my mother ahead of time.

"You know how to do macramé, don't you?"

"Some."

"Here's some leftover jute, if you want to work on a belt or something."

So I fooled around with the jute and finally settled on making a shoulder strap for the guitar I'm going to get some day. It was all very relaxed and nice, except that I was waiting to hear about plans for our trip to Wisdom Peak. I was about to go ahead and ask, but Charlotte got her question in first. "Heard from your father lately?"

"Yeah. We went to his place for dinner yesterday."

"You *did?* Come on, tell me about it."

"Well, he has an apartment over a warehouse in Stanhope. So far there's hardly any furniture in it, except a water bed."

"Jack Poindexter has a *water bed?*"

"Yes, and he also has a girl friend who writes children's books. She cooked a complete Indian dinner, curry and chutney and all, and afterward we let Allison beat us at Parcheesi."

"Wow! That's a lot of news! Did you say her last name?"

"Libby, he calls her. I don't remember the rest."

Charlotte was grinning and looking as though she might explode with curiosity and the humor of it all, but I didn't want to talk about Dad and/or Libby. So I paid a lot of attention to my half-hitches. While we knotted my aunt told me about her pottery class and about wedging and centering and pinching and slab building. "The students are merely so-so, most of them bored housewives looking for something to do to keep their hands busy. But the teacher is fantastic."

And then I couldn't stand it any longer. "Have you heard from Michael recently?" I asked, trying to sound casual, copying her tone when she asked about my father.

"Just got a letter Saturday. Let you read it soon as I finish this row of knots. Matter of fact, you can get it now if you want to dig through those papers on the shelf."

"Is he expecting us over spring vacation, does he say?" Because I couldn't wait even thirty more seconds to read the letter myself.

Charlotte looked surprised and then embarrassed. "Oh-hh, C.C., didn't I tell you? I'm going to Washington that week to represent our district at the Feminist Craftspersons Colloquium."

I felt as though a soyburger was stuck in my throat. I swallowed, but it stayed. I couldn't answer. I shook my head.

"C.C., I'm sorry. But we'll go as soon as school is out. In June. That's a *promise*. Cross my heart." And she crossed it.

"Okay," I said when the soyburger got unstuck. Then

I read Michael's letter, which was about how the fruit trees were going to bloom soon and planting was about to begin, and how he was helping to set up a darkroom, and about a new arrival named Tania who had made quite an impression on him.

Charlotte and I cleaned up the dishes and worked some more on the knots. Then she helped me lift my bike into the back of the all-purpose van and drove me home. I managed to sound quite cheerful when I said thanks and good night.

The kitchen was spotless. Allison had probably weaseled out of the dishes again, and my mother had done them for her. Near starvation, I located a tiny saucer of leftover lasagne; the rest must have gone into the freezer. I ate by the light of the open refrigerator. I could hear the Fact Finders in the living room, from which my mother called, "Shut that refrigerator door, please!" When I did, I saw a note in my mother's printing: "Laura called."

It was the first time she had phoned me since we agreed that telephones were to be used for emergency communication only. I dialed the Montgomerys' number and somebody answered after only one ring. At first I didn't recognize Laura's voice. "They're splitting," she said. "An irreconcilable breakdown of the marriage."

Another Situation for the ledger, obviously, but I couldn't think who it could be that was so important she'd call and tell me. Laura was beginning to take her ledger too seriously.

"Who this time?" I asked.

"Lois and Fred. They're selling our house. Everything is all arranged. They worked it all out, lawyers and everything. And I didn't know what was happening. They told me yesterday, but I didn't really believe them." She started to cry and hung up.

I crawled into bed and lay there thinking about Laura's problems and my own problems, like Wisdom Peak and my father and so on. And then I remembered that I had left the bead curtain at Charlotte's. That really bothered me for some reason, and I curled up and bawled as hard as Allison ever did.

Chapter Five

 I lay on the guest bunk in the sleeping area of Laura's room, watching her sort everything she owned. My feet hung out over the end of the bunk, because it had not been designed for guests who are over six feet tall. Packing boxes and plastic trash bags were arranged on the floor, and Laura was rapidly emptying the closets and drawers and methodically dropping each thing she picked up into the proper container. She worked fast because she doesn't get sentimental about possessions. The trash bags filled up quickly and the boxes were neatly packed.

The Montgomerys had sold their house after they decided to get a friendly divorce. They were going to continue as partners in their architectural firm, but they had decided that sharing a business and a marriage was too much. "It's easier to get a divorce than to dissolve a partnership," Laura said in her too-easy way that made it sound funny. I knew it was different because I had seen how hurt and upset she was back in the spring when she first found out and couldn't talk about it even to me.

Fred had remodeled the top floor of the building in the center of town where they had their offices and made it into an apartment. Laura said he decorated it with rare, fragile Louis the Fourteenth antiques, since he was sick of having everything built in around him. His new place resembled a small museum, and Laura called him the Curator.

Lois, on the other hand, was renovating an old barn on the edge of town, and she was filling it with countrified furniture featuring pine knots and splinters. She did this, she told Laura, to get in touch with her roots, because some of her ancestors had been farmers.

"Lois bought a spinning wheel," Laura said. "Great big old thing, really beautiful in a way. But since she still believes everything should have a function, she can't just put it next to the kitchen fireplace because she likes the way it looks there. So she wants me to take spinning lessons from some woman she's met, and then I can sit out there and spin and she can tell everyone, especially herself, 'Oh, Laura spins, you know.' And she wants to get some sheep, so it will be really authentic."

I flipped over on my stomach because the circulation in my legs was being cut off by the end of the bunk. "So are you going to spin?"

"Have you ever watched anybody spin? It's got to be the slowest and most boring thing in the world. And then, you know, you still don't have anything until you weave the yarn or knit it or something. Forget it! Can't you just picture me? Almost as ridiculous as Lois playing shepherdess."

I got a quick mental picture of Laura's mother, a sleek woman who dresses like a fashion model, suddenly transformed into a barefoot peasant and Laura, in a similar costume, spinning side by side at the hearth. We both started to laugh, and we kept on laughing because it felt so good. We hadn't been doing much of that lately.

The Shepherdess and the Curator had agreed on joint custody of Laura, who was supposed to divide her time between the two of them. They had worked out a complicated schedule of which days and which weekends and which holidays and which vacations Laura would spend with whom, but Laura flatly refused to go along with their plan. "I told them I'd divide my time between them, but it had to be the way it worked out best for me." Since the Montgomerys believed in giving children a lot of freedom and responsibility from a very young age, they had to agree. "So I'll just work it out as I go along and see what happens. After all, none of this was my idea in the first place."

It sounded fine, and that's probably what Fred and Lois had agreed to, but I knew Laura better than that, even if her parents didn't. Laura never just worked things out as she went along. She was a long-range planner by instinct.

When the packing was finished we went down to the kitchen to find something to eat. Mildred wasn't there—she too had been divided in a joint custody agreement and was to spend three days a week with each of the Montgomerys. But she didn't like the idea either, and she quit before the agreement went into effect. The kitchen seemed empty and somehow dismal without her. "It doesn't seem right without Mildred here to tell us how bad things are," I said.

"You know, that miserable woman knew about the divorce long before I did? I mean, the *housekeeper* had figured out exactly what was going on." Laura shook her head at the unfathomable mystery of it all.

"Yes, but she specializes in gossipy bad news," I said, trying to soothe her.

"So do I," she said.

There were no quiches in the freezer, but there was still a jar of liver paté and some calamari and a tiny can containing two truffles. We ate it all up, being deliberately messy, but it wasn't much fun without Mildred there to complain and nag. We both knew this was kind of a farewell dinner in that house, and I didn't want to think about that. My life stayed pretty much the same when my parents split, but Laura's was changing completely.

It was time for me to go home. Laura walked me out to the end of her driveway. "What I really want," she said in a low voice, "is my own apartment."

"That's a great idea. I wouldn't mind something like that myself. Maybe we could each have one, with connecting doors or something."

"I'm serious. You're not."

I could see that. "So now what?"

"I'm not sure, beyond a certain point. I'll shuffle back and forth between Fred and Lois for a while, and then they'll sort of lose track of where I am and go back to whatever it is they're doing, and I'll be free."

"Money," I reminded her.

"I'd have to get a job, but it would be worth it."

"Nobody rents an apartment to a kid."

"I'll figure something out," she said, and I knew from that tone of voice she probably would. She turned then and walked back up the drive and I pedaled slowly home.

There was a message for me clapped to the refrigerator door with a tiny magnetic apple. "Call your aunt." My Aunt Charlotte? I went to find my mother. She was reading in bed. "Do you mean Charlotte?"

"Do you have any other aunts?"

"But she never calls. Did she say what she wanted?"

"She never tells me anything."

I went back out to the kitchen and dialed, although I thought it must be a mistake and that she would not answer. But she did, and first we had a little chat about Laura and how she was doing. Then she plunged in. "C.C., I know how much you counted on the trip to Wisdom Peak, I know how badly you want to go, and I feel just awful disappointing you for a second time after I had *promised*." And crossed her heart. "But I have just gotten the most fabulous chance to spend the summer at an artists' colony in Massachusetts. . . ." And she kept on telling me about the place and how she had been on the waiting list for months and had never dreamed that she would be accepted, and if it hadn't been for a cancellation she wouldn't have gone until next year, and she had in fact not even known the possibility had existed when she had promised we'd go to Wisdom Peak. She kept on talking, half-excited because of being accepted at the colony, half-embarrassed because she was letting me down.

When she stopped talking I said, "Hey, Charlotte, it's okay. It really is. I'm not mad, and I'm not even that disappointed." Even though she had crossed her heart.

Big sigh of relief: I had let her off the hook, and she didn't have to feel guilty. "I hadn't even gotten around to asking my mother if I could go," I told her. Partly because

I figured my mother would say no and partly because I figured Charlotte didn't really mean to go anyway, I just kept putting off asking. I had begun to develop a sense of what was going to work out for me and what wasn't.

For the next couple of weeks I lived in a kind of fog. It was the end of the term, and we were all involved in getting papers finished and completing projects and studying for exams. I didn't see much of Laura, except in the cafeteria. She always had funny stories to tell about the Curator and the Shepherdess and how neither one of them ever seemed to know where she was. I didn't see Charlotte, either, since she also had a lot to do to finish up her courses and get organized for her summer at the artists' colony. My mother suddenly stopped going to bed every night at eight o'clock; she had met a man named Alex McChesney, and everything seemed to hang on whether Alex called or didn't call. He had a nice English accent and he seemed okay, but I didn't really think about him much.

After my last exam I stopped by the art room to say hello and good-bye to Charlotte. The room was a gigantic glass oven. The air-conditioning was not strong enough to counteract the effects of the sun on all those big glass windows. Somebody from Central Maintenance had tried to put up some kind of blinds near the top of the big windows, but they didn't do much good and they always hung crooked and looked terrible.

The room was almost empty. All the easels and other equipment had been packed away, the Bunny Bed was gone, and Charlotte was cleaning out her desk drawers. She had her hair pulled up on top of her head and wound into a little knot, but lots of little straggly hairs floated around her sweaty face. She dropped into a chair when she saw me and waved for me to sit down, too. We rested in silence for a minute. You could hardly breathe.

"Hey, let's get out of here," she said. "I've got a proposition for you, but it's too hot to talk. I'm done here anyway." She took another look in her desk drawers and slammed them all shut. Then we each picked up a cardboard carton to carry out to the van. The parking lot was nearly empty. There was a whip-thin maple tree by the tennis courts where the van was parked, and we sprawled under it in sight of the huge school building. The new wing of the high school which included the art room had won some kind of prize for architecture, but Charlotte said it was a disaster that had cost the taxpayers about half a million dollars.

"Nobody fusses about *that*," she said.

What they were fussing about was the Bunny Bed. "Voice of the People" had just published another long letter about the art department, stating that the Bunny Bed was not anybody's idea of art and that it was probably obscene and the teacher was probably immoral. Charlotte had had the clipping blown up into a poster which she hung on the wall behind her desk, next to a photograph of Mr. McDermott pretending to be asleep on the Bunny Bed. The poster was on top of one of the cartons we had just put in the van. The photograph must have been packed inside.

"Now here is my idea," she said. "Matter of fact, I've been intending to call you, but things have really been wild." She slipped into one of her yoga positions that made my joints ache just to watch. "I'm leaving for Massachusetts Sunday morning, if I can get it all together by then, which I think I can. That gives me tomorrow and maybe part of the next day to pack. I've called my friend Moozy—remember her? from the rap group?"—I did—"at Country and Seashore Real Estate to see if she can rent the house to somebody, but of course that's a problem because of Hugo, unless I put him in a kennel, which would cost more than I'd get in rent. And break his poor heart. Also the house needs a thorough cleaning before anyone moves in, and even if no one does, the refrigerator has to be cleaned out and so on, and I know for sure I don't have that kind of time.

"Then there's the garden which I just put in, and that should be tended. And Hugo has to be fed and taken for a walk twice a day. Now Moozy says there are house sitting services that can do all of that, and she says she'll arrange for one, but I'm thinking that it's a job you could handle if you wanted to. I'd pay you for it, of course. Even if the place does get rented, which it might, but might not, you'd still have some work to do in the garden. Not much, just watering if it's a dry summer. I've got everything mulched. And of course making sure Hugo is okay. But what do you think? Do you want that kind of a job?"

The first thing that came into my head was what my mother would say: "Obviously she has never seen your room." And then I thought that even though it was not my idea of a terrific summer job, it was better than nothing. But she hadn't said anything about money, and while I was thinking how to ask her, she said, "I'll pay you the price of a bus ticket to Wisdom Peak. That's minimum. But keep track of the time you actually put in, and we'll work out the rest when I get back. I don't quite know how to pay you—look, I don't want to be bothered sending you money every week, so I'll just give you a hundred dollars now, and if you think you should get more in the mean-time, just write and say so. Or if somebody moves in next week and wants to take care of Hugo and the garden and you find yourself suddenly unemployed, just buy the bus ticket and keep some spending money, and return whatever's left, if there is any. I still feel bad about letting you down."

Wisdom Peak looked a lot closer and more real than it had before. This time I wouldn't be depending on somebody doing a favor to get me there.

In a couple of hours it was all arranged. I went to Charlotte's with her in the van and followed her around making notes and lists of what had to be done. As I followed Charlotte, Hugo followed me. I could see that people might think he looked scary, because of his size. He might kill you with affection, but that was all. My mother said it was foolish to keep a big dog that was so expensive to feed, but Charlotte was quite attached to him. My mother also pointed out that having a dog of any size whatsoever took away your freedom almost as much as a child did. This was the argument my mother always used against getting us a dog. We could always say that we would feed it and take care of it and clean up after it (she never believed any of those promises), but there was nothing we could say about who would take care of it if we went away. Our argument that we never went anywhere, anyway, didn't mean anything because there was always the chance that we *might*, and there would not even be that chance if we had a dog for my mother to worry about.

"And don't forget to water the plants. Actually you can put most of them outside in the shade." She went on to explain about how to dig a hole and put the pot in that, and so on. One thing I didn't have to worry about was renting the place. Moozy had a set of keys, and she would take care of everything. Charlotte would tell Moozy to keep in touch with me, so I'd know what was going on. But probably nothing would happen because of Hugo. I didn't suggest that I could take Hugo home with me, since I knew what my mother would say. So did Charlotte, because she didn't suggest it either.

I helped my aunt load her canvases into the van and watched her pack her wardrobe of black pants and shirts into a big suitcase. We wrestled her bicycle up on the roof of the van and tied it down. All the time she was getting her gear organized, she was still remembering things to tell me. "Want to stay for supper and eat up whatever's left in the refrigerator?" I figured it would be leftover soybean something, and I just couldn't face it, so after we thought we had everything organized she drove me home. "I guess I ought to tell your mother what's going on," she said.

"Yeah, I guess so."

But when we got there the car was gone and the house was empty.

"Well, I made the effort," Charlotte said. "Listen, C.C., I'll give you a buzz before I leave. And you've got the money and my address and phone number, in case you need to get in touch with me. I hope you don't. I don't think you will. Write, though, and let me know how it's going."

I promised to write every week.

"Good woman," she said.

We gave each other a hug. Charlotte is the only person besides my father who hugs me and I hug back. Then she jumped into the van and drove away, beeping the horn twice at the end of the driveway.

Sunday, the day Charlotte left for Massachusetts, my father took us to the beach for what he called a family picnic. The family consisted of my father, my sister, and me, plus Libby and her three children, Scott, Billy, and Jennifer. This was our long-awaited get-together. Our two-car caravan finally arrived at Nesbitt Beach State Park about eleven a.m., by which time practically everybody else in the county plus all those people who started out from New York City at dawn had grabbed all the parking places close to the beach and all the wooden picnic tables and grills. Our plan had been to get there early too, but we weren't exactly well organized. Not that Libby didn't try.

We managed to find a warped picnic table covered with bird droppings about a mile from the parking lot and also from the building where you change clothes, go to the bathroom, and buy refreshments. Everybody had to carry something. Libby had packed two big hampers of food and a basket with tablecloth, plates, silverware, and so on, as though we were eating at home. This was not to be the usual hot dog and hamburger cookout. My father had to lug a cast iron hibachi all the way from the parking lot. Allison dragged a bag of charcoal, grumbling every step of the way.

Libby's oldest kid, Scott, was snotty and morose. He smoked cigarettes in front of his mother, taking them from my father's pack without asking and arguing with everything anyone said. Libby had explained that Scott had problems. He is in psychotherapy, but meanwhile we must all be careful and understanding and forgiving. I had been careful and understanding and forgiving for about two hours, and I would have liked to bust him in the chops.

Nobody paid much attention to Billy. He has big eyes and large knobby knees and elbows. He's skinny, almost starved looking, and very quiet. I taught him to play double solitaire and he sat beside me silently, waiting for me to propose another game.

Jennifer is ten, the same age as Allison. She is pretty and fragile looking, and she whines a lot. I have thought for years that Allison is a royal pain, but I believe Jennifer is actually worse. Allison had been working up to a tantrum all day. She was always either working up to one, having one, getting over one, or taking a breather between. During the breathers she seemed almost pleasant and civilized.

"When do we eat?" Allison wanted to know. We were all weak with hunger, but first the fire had to be built and then the little rock cornish game hens had to be roasted on spits over the charcoal. Dad was struggling to get the fire going. He had forgotten the lighter fluid, and the charcoal would not catch.

"First the charcoal has to turn gray," Libby explained. "That takes about a half-hour. Then the birds have to roast for about an hour. Plenty of time for you all to have a good swim before we eat. Then you'll have a good appetite worked up."

"I don't need an appetite worked up. I've got one now."

"You might as well start on these, then," Libby said, handing Allison a platter on which raw carrots, celery sticks, cucumber slices, radishes cut to resemble roses, cauliflower chunks, and mushrooms were arranged like a small flower garden. Allison stared at the garden and passed it to Jennifer. Hunger was preferable to raw vegetables.

Scott was assigned to scrub the table with a sponge brought by Libby especially for the purpose, but he had disappeared. So I did it, and after it had dried I set the table with the green and white checkered cloth and what seemed to be a complete set of yellow dishes and coordinated yellow mugs and green napkins. I lined up the silverware next to each plate and stood back to admire the effect. It looked quite festive, I thought. Allison hung around making little noises and sighing heavily.

"Go for a swim and forget about food for a while," my father said impatiently, blowing gently on the little flame he had finally coaxed into the little pile of charcoal.

"Where do we change?" Allison wanted to know.

"Didn't you wear your bathing suit? You have to walk to the bathhouse, all the way back there."

"That's too far," Allison said.

"Come on, Allison, I'll go with you," I said, even though I had my suit on under my cut-off jeans.

While Allison was getting changed I bought us each a hamburger and loaded it with ketchup and mustard and pickle relish, which was one thing we both agreed on. We had each taken the first huge bite when Jennifer strolled out of the bathroom. It was too late to hide the food. "I'm telling," she said.

"Don't bother, Jennifer," I said. "I'll get you one, too." The three of us hitched up onto a wooden railing and watched the gulls diving for garbage. We were ready to start back when I noticed that Allison had dripped ketchup and mustard and pickle relish down the front of her pink bathing suit. "You better get that cleaned off,"

I told her. "Everybody will know you've been eating. And it looks terrible."

"Sloppy, isn't she?" Jennifer observed in a superior tone as we waited for Allison to clean up. A lovely child, I thought. While we were walking back, the two girls jabbering away to each other as though they were long-time friends, a stone whizzed past my ear. I turned fast and saw Scott lounging against a tree.

Jennifer saw him, too. "Don't worry," she said soothingly, "he hardly ever hits anything he's aiming at." Then she danced over to her brother. "Guess what, Scotty. I just had a hamburger. C.C. bought it for me." She turned back to me. "You'd better get him one, too. Or he'll get us all in trouble."

I was beginning to detest this family. They all waited while I went back and bought him his hamburger.

"You must be the tallest freakin' female I've ever seen," Scott said almost admiringly.

Here we go again, I thought. "Not quite," I told him, "but I'm working on it." I gave him his hamburger. Neither of Libby's carefully trained children said thank you. "Where's Billy?" I asked them. Nobody knew. I had bought him a bag of potato chips.

When we got back the charcoal was glowing and Libby and Dad had rigged up the little hens on some sort of spit. Someone had to go and turn and baste them every few minutes, and we were to take turns doing this. Then we all trooped down to the water. It was frigid, as it always is until at least the Fourth of July. There weren't more than a dozen people out there. We went in, though, at least partway. All except Libby, who never took off the long flowered dress and big floppy hat she had come in.

99

"It's much too cold for me," she said, and she settled in a beach chair with her sunglasses and a stack of books, which she underlined and made notes in as she read. My father, who is a good swimmer and is normally unfazed by either air or water temperature, lay on a towel next to her, baking in the hot sun. Libby was obsessed with those game hens, and every few minutes she would go running back to do something to them.

Allison and Jennifer said the water was too cold, and they squatted on the beach just beyond the reach of the little lapping waves and began to build an elaborate system of ditches and walls in the wet sand. Then Scott ambled over and kicked at their project and splashed them until they cried. When Billy wandered by with his collection of pretty stones, Scott grabbed him by his skinny arm and demanded a share of the potato chips which Billy did not yet know I had bought for him. I went to get him his chips and to try to protect him from Scott and narrowly escaped being discovered by Libby on another chicken-basting trip.

Lunch was finally ready at about two o'clock. The table looked like a picture from a food magazine, with everything artistically arranged and decorated with sprigs of parsley. An artichoke sat at each place; next to it was a little white paper cup of sauce. Libby and Dad sat on one side of the table, hemmed in on each end of the bench by Libby's boys. I took the opposite side, planning to sit in the middle to keep peace between Jennifer and Allison. But they both insisted they wanted to be next to each other, and I surrendered my place.

Jennifer airily began to eat her artichoke, pulling one leaf at a time daintily between her teeth to scrape off the green flesh. Then she placed the leaf in a neat pattern on her plate. Allison, who had never eaten an artichoke and had probably never even seen one before, was busily attacking her game hen, but she put down the bird and stared at Jennifer. I expected her to say "Yuk" which she does to any ordinary vegetable, but she seemed fascinated. She abandoned the hen and attacked her artichoke instead. She yanked off the leaves with great flourishes, dunked up globs of sauce, sucked it off the leaf without eating any of the green flesh, and laid the leaf on her plate. She pretended that she had been eating artichokes every day for years.

Jennifer stared at her in disgust. "You're not even eating your artichoke," she said. "Mother, Allison isn't eating the green part. She's just licking off the sauce."

"I am so eating it."

"You are not. I'll bet you've never eaten an artichoke before in your whole life, or you'd know how to do it correctly."

"I have too! I do so!"

"Jennifer, dear, let Allison eat it however she wants to."

"I think she ought to do it right."

Meanwhile, Allison had run out of sauce. "More of that mayonnaise, please," she said, ignoring her critic.

"It's not *may*onnaise, it's *holl*andaise," Jennifer told her with a sniff. "And if you ate correctly you wouldn't need more."

Allison got very red in the face. The tantrum that had been coming all day was ready to break. "Shut the hell up," she said, "before I punch you in your damn mouth."

101

"Allison!" said my father, sounding shocked, because he had apparently forgotten about her tantrums.

"Mother, this girl has no manners at *all*," Jennifer whined, beginning to sniffle.

"They're a hell of a lot better than yours," growled Allison.

"Allison!" my father said again. "Allison, leave the table *right now!*"

People at the next table were staring. Allison, victim of injustice, insulted without possibility of retaliation, at least at that moment, began to howl. Roaring and spluttering, she tried to leave, but she was stuck between Jennifer and me on our side of the bench. When she managed to pull one foot over the bench, her sneaker brushed rather hard against Jennifer, maybe not quite by accident.

"Ohhh, she kicked me! Mother, did you see?"

"Allison, I do think you owe Jennifer an apology."

"Yes, Allison, for God's sake," my father added.

It was too much. My sister straddled the bench, blinking at Libby and Dad lined up side by side against her. Jennifer looked like a haughtily suffering princess, and Scott was actually grinning for the first time. Billy slowly gnawed a piece of garlic bread. Allison hesitated for only a second. She grabbed Jennifer's little paper cup of hollandaise, which was still three-quarters full because Jennifer has had so much practice in making the leaves and sauce come out even, and she slapped it upside down on top of Jennifer's head. "You got a head like a artichoke," Allison sobbed, yanking out her other foot and stumbling toward the beach.

Jennifer began screaming with rage. Scott was screaming with laughter. Billy began giggling nervously. I started dabbing with my napkin at the yellowish stuff in Jennifer's dark hair. She shrieked, "Don't you dare touch me!" Libby reached across the table, upsetting her mug of red wine. The stain seeped slowly over the tablecloth. Libby picked up another napkin and started to mop up the wine, and Jennifer howled, "What about *me?*"

Scott, choking on his food, cackled, "You got a head like a artichoke!"

"Hush," Libby croaked hoarsely. "What's wrong with all of you?"

Dad apparently decided not to chase Allison, and he sat down on the bench again. "Let's just leave everybody alone for a while. What did you do with the wine?"

"Jack, you can't ignore situations like this. You have to deal with them as they come up."

"I can deal with most things better when I've had a nice glass of wine and something to eat." He began searching through the hampers for the wine bottle, which had to be kept out of sight because alcoholic beverages are not permitted in the park, even for gourmet picnics like ours.

"When the situation develops, that's the time to deal with it," Libby said, paying no attention to his request for wine. I had a pretty good idea where it was; Scott had slipped it out of the hamper while they were fussing at Allison. Suddenly my father picked up the half-naked artichoke from his own plate and plopped it down on Libby's along with the container of sauce.

"Forgive me, love, but I've never learned to eat artichokes either."

Time to get out of here, I decided. I picked up the rest of my game hen and some garlic bread and walked down to the beach. Allison and Jennifer were both there, looking relatively peaceful. In fact they were working on their wall-and-ditch project again, from opposite sides, without speaking. They were scowling, but not much. Scott had a soft drink bottle filled with something dark red. Billy was sitting on the sand, hugging his knobby knees, staring unhappily at the water. The sun was very hot.

"Let's go for a swim," I suggested.

"Not for an hour after we've eaten," said Jennifer importantly.

"You didn't eat that much," Allison told her.

"Nobody got to eat anything!" Billy complained.

"All because of Allison," Jennifer declared, nasty again.

The effect was immediate. Allison called Jennifer a few choice names, Dopey Nut Face for starters. She is very inventive. Jennifer was not up to this, and her royal feelings were injured, even though she had certainly asked for it. She started to cry noisily. Our father appeared suddenly from among the trees. "Get your gear collected. We're leaving."

"I'm still hungry," Allison whined.

"Aren't you going to take us out in a boat like you promised, Uncle Jack?" Jennifer wheedled with a coy smile.

"No. Next time. If you behave."

"Ha," Scott contributed. He sat in a tree, cradling the pop bottle which was now only half-filled. Dad glared at him but did not notice the wine or else pretended not to.

We collected our stuff—or most of it, because Allison left a towel behind, as usual—and put it in the trunk of Dad's car. In the parking space next to ours, Libby was packing hampers and baskets into the trunk of *her* car. They did their packing in silence. Allison and Jennifer were busy making faces at each other from the back seats of their separate cars. Jennifer was much better at it than Allison, whose specialty is unusual name-calling. One of the faces was particularly grotesque, and Allison broke up laughing. Then Jennifer leaned out of her window and yelled, "Hey, Allison, want to come over to my house and play some day?"

"Yeah! When?"

"I'll call you."

"Okay. Maybe I'll call *you!*"

"Okay! See you."

"Yeah, see you!"

Libby whipped her car out of the parking space without saying good-bye, but lots of other people were beginning to leave too, and progress toward the exit was slow. While we trailed along behind them, Jennifer made hideous faces and Scott flashed some obscene gestures.

"Hey, can I ride with them?" Allison pleaded.

"No."

"Can Jennifer ride with us, then?"

"No."

"Why not?"

"Because I said no," said my father wearily.

"I thought you two hated each other," I put in.

"Not really," Allison explained. "It's nice to have someone your own age to fight with."

Chapter Six

My mother leaned both elbows on the kitchen table and twisted a strand of hair around her finger. "I just had a job interview," she said. "They want to hire me." She didn't look too pleased.

"What kind of job is it?"

"Working for an engineering company."

"Doing what?"

"Little bit of everything. Answering the phone, typing invoices, processing shipping papers." She stopped fiddling with her hair and swirled what was left of a cup of coffee.

It sounded dull and awful, and I couldn't act very excited about it. But I wanted to be excited for her sake. When my father left, he promised to send her enough money until she could take some brush-up courses and find a job. Before I was born she had been an editorial assistant for a publisher of Italian books. It hadn't taken her long now to find out that there wasn't a lot of demand for that kind of experience; it was just as though she had never done anything at all. Then she enrolled in a business course and learned accounting procedures and how to use an electric typewriter and dictating machines and so on. She didn't like the course, but when she had finished it she was qualified to look for a job she wouldn't like either. And now she had found one.

"It sounds like a good way to meet people," I suggested.

She flicked me a glance. "The good part is that it's right near here. I could probably even walk there and save gas." She looked at me, very tired. "That's a dumb reason to take a job, isn't it?"

"We all have to start somewhere." Poindexter the Philosopher.

"Actually, I think your job as Charlotte's caretaker sounds more interesting."

When the phone rang, she jumped up to answer, even though I was standing next to it. I knew it had to be McChesney, because she immediately stopped looking tired and depressed. She told him about her job offer. The way she described it to McChesney it sounded interesting, important, and maybe even fun. "The salary isn't that great, Alex, but the diversity. . . ."

I took a walk into the living room. When I heard her hang up, I went back to the kitchen to look for something to eat.

"Alex is taking me out for dinner to celebrate my new job," she told me. "And then I'm going to help him with the Encore Singles newsletter. So will you please fix something for you and Allison to eat? There's some leftover chicken, I think, but maybe not enough, and . . . let's see . . ."

107

"Don't worry. I'll make my specialty, Macaroni Montage. Allie always likes that."

While Mom went to take a bath and do something about her hair, I cooked up a batch of macaroni and started adding whatever I could find in the refrigerator: cheese, naturally, and some odds and ends like creamed spinach and the chicken my mother mentioned and a slice of dried-up bologna, and some chunks of green pepper and a tomato that was going soft.

I was still fooling around with this, chopping onion and shaking in some herbs, when my mother appeared in a new brown African-print dress. She had on white sandals and big white hoop earrings and looked very nice. Sexy, even. Mrs. Panek's advice was either beginning to have an effect, or a man can make an awful lot of difference in a woman's life. Maybe both.

Mr. McChesney arrived exactly on time. He had gray hair getting thin on top and deep lines around his mouth and baggy eyelids. They made him look a bit beaglish. He talked with what I thought was an English accent, but my mother explained he was Australian. While we were standing around making polite conversation, and Mr. McChesney was inquiring about my recipe for Macaroni Montage, Allison came tramping in. I stopped describing the concoction so she could be introduced.

"Do you have any children?" Allison asked while they were shaking hands.

"Yes, indeed," he said. "I have a son Douglas who is away at school and a daughter Belinda who will be thirteen in September. Maybe we could all get together some day soon. For a picnic, perhaps. What do you say to that? Wouldn't it be fun?"

Allison groaned. "Oh, my Lord, here we go again!"

"Allison!" my mother said, looking embarrassed. "That was a very rude thing to say to Mr. McChesney."

"I daresay she's had some unfortunate experiences," Mr. McChesney remarked with hearty good humor.

Mom didn't want to continue this conversation, and she began edging Mr. McChesney toward the door. "Be good, kids," she said. "In bed by nine thirty, Allison. I left emergency phone numbers on the refrigerator."

"When will you be back?" Allison wanted to know.

"After you're fast asleep, young lady," Mr. McChesney said firmly.

"Wanna bet?" Allison whispered so only I could hear.

After they were gone she watched gloomily while I piled the macaroni mixture into the buttered casserole. There was too much for the medium-sized casserole, but I didn't feel like dragging out the bigger one and greasing that one, too, so I just mounded it high in the middle and sprinkled crumbs and chunks of butter over the top. There was enough to feed a large family. "What's in it?" Allison asked.

"I won't tell you. Professional secret. You might give it away."

"Then I won't eat it." Allison had no sense of humor.

"Fine. Starve then."

"You're mean."

"All cooks are mean. Sometimes they roast bratty little sisters."

"My friend Diana is having roast beef tonight, and chocolate cake for dessert."

"Terrific. Did she invite you?"

"Yes."

"Then go, by all means."

Allison took off to talk Diana's mother into issuing the invitation—I was pretty sure she had not already—and I put my masterpiece into the oven. I was thinking what a shame it was that all this marvelous food was not going to be shared, and if I didn't have some help I would probably eat the whole thing single-handedly. If I could find Laura and get her to come over to help eat it, I could tell her about my job as summer caretaker for Charlotte's place. My mother was out celebrating her new job; I was entitled to celebrate mine, too.

Since the Montgomerys had split and Laura was shuttling between both parents, I didn't see much of her. I also wasn't sure where to get in touch with her. I dialed the Shepherdess's number. The ringing was interrupted by an answering machine with a recording of Lois's voice saying that she was sorry to miss my call and would I please leave a message at the sound of the tone. But before the tone sounded, the real Lois cut in over the recording. "Laura isn't here, which must mean she's at Fred's," she said. "But in case she's not, I'll tell her you called."

The Curator didn't have an answering machine. He had an answering service, run by a real person. But the real person was in no hurry and on the sixth ring Laura answered in a French accent pitched about an octave below her normal voice. "Allo? Oui?"

"I've made my Macaroni Montage, and there's nobody here to eat it with me. I also have some interesting news. Can you come?"

"Oui. Immediatement." And she hung up.

A celebration ought to be done up in style, I thought, so while I waited for Laura to bike two miles out from the middle of town, I set the dining room table with my mother's good china, the monogrammed silver, the cut crystal goblets, and the embroidered linen placemats with matching napkins. None of it had been used in well over a year. I even remembered to lay out a silver serving spoon and a silver trivet for the casserole. It was tarnished, but there was no time for polishing it now. When I saw Laura come wheeling up the driveway, I lit the candles in the silver candelabra.

"What monstrous middle-class pretentiousness," Laura said approvingly. "I brought the dessert." She fished two packages of somewhat deformed cream-filled Twinkies from the pockets of her denim shirt, and I arranged them on a little silver plate.

My mother didn't allow sodas in the house, but I found part of a can of strawberry mix on a top shelf where my sister had hidden and forgotten it, and we added that to the milk and stirred it in the crystal goblets.

Then I brought my beautiful casserole to the table. There was one slight problem: it had been too full, and a lot of the juice had run over and was burned on the bottom of the oven. I made a mental note to clean it when I did the dishes.

We served each other huge helpings. "It's grotesque," Laura said, polishing off one plateful and reaching for another. "You should franchise it, like fried chicken. You'd make a fortune."

"I'm already making a fortune," I said, which wasn't at all the case, but it was a good opening. Then I told her about Charlotte going to the artists' colony for the summer, and how I was looking after her house and taking care of Hugo and getting paid at least enough to finance a trip to Wisdom Peak on my own. "The only bad part is that I have to clean house for her, in case the house gets rented."

What was going through my mind was that I might be able to talk Laura into helping me, because she is a naturally very neat and well-organized person. That turned out to be nothing compared to what was apparently going through Laura's mind at the same instant.

"The house isn't rented yet, then."

"No, but Charlotte has a friend in the real estate business who's trying to find somebody. What makes it hard is that Hugo is part of the deal, and not everybody wants to spend a summer with a Saint Bernard."

"Listen, C.C., we've got to make *sure* nobody wants to spend the summer with Hugo."

"How come?" My brain was running about ten steps behind Laura's as usual.

"Because that place is the perfect answer. Don't you see? I can live there all summer. I'll clean the place and do the gardening and take care of Hugo and everything. Once a week I'll pay a visit to Fred and Lois, if they're around. They're so busy they'll never figure out that I'm not with the other one. I'll do all the work, and you'll get paid for it. It's a perfect deal. All *you* have to do is make sure nobody rents the place."

"Look, I don't think I can do that."

"Why not?"

"Just can't, that's all. I mean, I don't think my aunt would like it."

"She'd never know. And to be quite frank, C.C., you know I'd do a better job of cleaning than you would. Also it would be better if Hugo had company and wasn't there by himself all the time."

I couldn't really argue with that. Except that I knew Charlotte was really hoping to get some money from renting the house. Even if I could somehow keep the house from being rented, so that Laura could stay there, it would be like stealing. Which I carefully explained while we polished off the rest of about a gallon of Macaroni Montage.

"You're right," she said, "ethically and morally. So let me suggest this: let's be fatalistic and say, 'What will be, will be.' I'll do all the cleaning, as I said, and I'll take care of Hugo and the garden until somebody rents it. You don't have to do a thing to prevent it. Somebody comes, I go. *Que sera, sera.*"

The way she put it, I couldn't see anything wrong. In fact it was beginning to sound like a perfect situation. "It's a deal," I said.

"Let's go over there right now," Laura said, halfway through her first Twinkie.

"The dishes," I protested feebly.

"We'll do them afterwards. How long does it take to dash over there and say hello to Hugo and come right back?"

I got the keys and we grabbed our bikes and took off. Somehow the house seemed creepily quiet as we pushed open the door, even with Hugo bounding out to meet us. Just to make it seem less like we were breaking and entering, I lit some candles and put a record on the stereo. Charlotte is the only adult I know who has any understanding of what people my age enjoy in the way of music. Then we went carefully through the house, starting in the kitchen. There wasn't much in the refrigerator, just some containers of homemade yogurt and some sprouts and cooked soybeans, but the cupboards looked like the shelves of a health food store—carob powder, brown rice, sesame seeds, blackstrap molasses. And dogfood. Hugo is not a vegetarian.

Next we checked the Meditation Room, which was almost empty again because Charlotte had taken all of her canvases with her. Laura was fascinated with the bathroom, because my aunt prepares most of her own cosmetics. She says toothpaste is a fraud, so she keeps a mixture of salt and baking powder in a shaker. And she buys whole coconuts and cooks the meat to extract the oil, which she uses as a base for her face cream.

I showed Laura the trapdoor that led to the attic space above the Meditation Room. I was in favor of leaving that for another time, but Laura wouldn't quit until she'd checked every inch of what she now saw as her home. She brought a stool from the kitchen and climbed on that, but she still couldn't reach the trapdoor. I could, but the catch was stuck. Finally we gave up. "Plenty of time for that later," she said.

Finally we shut off the stereo, made sure again that Hugo had enough food and water and had had his belly rubbed. It was nearly dark when we left. We had stayed much longer than we planned. "Hey, I don't like to stick you with the dishes at your house, but I've really got to get over to Fred's. He worries more."

"It's okay," I said. "They won't be home until late, I don't think."

"I'll come over tomorrow," she said. "And move in." She flicked on her generator light, and I followed her up the winding driveway. We rode along together for a while, and then she turned right toward town and I went left toward my house. A minute later I heard the squawk of her horn and she pedaled up furiously. "You forgot to give me the keys." I handed them over and we said good night again.

Every light was blazing when I got home, and Mr. McChesney's car was parked by the kitchen door. I walked my bike along the grass and eased it into the garage. Then I tiptoed softly up the cellar stairs and into the kitchen. Allison greeted me with a whoop that would wake the dead. "Hoo, boy, are you ever in trouble!"

"How come?"

"Because when I came home from Diana's you weren't here, so I called Mama at the restaurant and they had gone already and then at Mr. McChesney's, and she and him came right away and found all the china and silver and glasses and stuff on the table, which you are not allowed to use, and that you went off and left me all alone here by myself—"

"You weren't even here."

"Doesn't matter. Mama says you're totally irresponsible. You were supposed to be taking care of me, and you went and left me and what if something bad had happened?"

"You'd deserve it," I said, and I went into the living room to take my bawling out, which I knew would not be too terrible since Mr. McChesney was there.

The next morning, after I had cleaned up the mess from my dinner party, including the oven and in addition the refrigerator which was extra duty because of the night before, I dressed up in a skirt and blouse (one that was neither ripped nor stained) and shoes and pulled my hair

115

into a twist which makes me look quite mature. Then I borrowed a purse of my mother's, stuck it in the saddle bag of my bike, and pedaled out Kings Highway to the shopping plaza. In a quaint Victorian house across from the plaza were the offices of Country and Seashore Real Estate, identified by a sign lettered in Olde English script. All the really nice antique houses around our town have been turned into real estate offices or funeral parlors, which gives you an idea of what the main concerns are. I parked my bike behind the house and hurried inside before I could lose my nerve.

The receptionist stopped giggling into the company telephone and gazed up at me. One thing about being very tall is that people often take you for being much older than you actually are. I pulled the business card Charlotte had given me out of the pocket of my blouse. Under the name of the firm, printed in the same Olde English script, it said, "Baroness M. von Schmidt, rental representative."

"May I see Baroness von Schmidt, please?" I said formally to the receptionist. She looked about my age, also pretending to be older.

"And who may I say is calling?" she recited.

"Ms. Poindexter."

She spoke into her telephone mouthpiece, which was suspended almost invisibly in front of her face on a wire that emerged from behind her left ear. "Pam? Listen, I'll call you later, okay? Somebody here." Then she punched another button on the phone, consulted a list beside her, and dialed. A phone rang in the next office. I could see the slice of blue carpet through the half-open door. If I had stepped three feet to the right I would have also been able to see the phone and the person who answered it. I heard the person punch the button on her phone and say, "Yes?" and then punch another button and say, "Yes?" again. That time she got it right. The receptionist announced, "A *Miz* Poindexter here to see you." Then the person in the other room said, "Tell her I'll be right out."

But before the receptionist could deliver the message, Moozy flung her door open the rest of the way and swept out of the blue-carpeted office. She didn't recognize me right away, probably because of my hairdo. "I'm C.C., Charlotte's niece," I explained.

"Darling! How perfectly delightful to see you again!" And she fluttered and wafted me into her office, where I settled into the visitor's seat, a wing chair not quite as large as the wing chair behind the antique desk.

"The rap group was responsible for all these changes," she said, waving vaguely around the office. She had begun a new life, she told me, an entirely new existence. When she had decided that she needed a job, her dear old friend Roger Hornberger had given her an office and a desk, which she had had replaced by her decorator who had also suggested the pale blue carpet and the antique desk with the white china lamp on it shaped like an urn, and a whole new collection of blue and yellow paintings on the wall, all in Moozy's personal style. She was even thinking of using her maiden name, but Roger had talked her out of it. He thought it was very high-class to have a baroness on the staff, much better than a Marie Snook, which was her maiden name. She agreed with him.

"Roger started me off with summer rentals," she said. "And your dear Aunt Charlotte is one of my first clients. I'm *very* anxious to get her somebody absolutely marvelous for her house. It's a little gem, isn't it? A perfect jewel. Actually I'd move in there in a minute myself —so quiet, so private, but quite convenient too, you know. There's just nothing comparable to it so close to town. Here, let me read you the ad I'm putting in the local papers—people from the city read these papers, you know, when they're looking for a summer place. Now just listen to this: 'FOR RENT, ARTIST'S HIDEAWAY. Studio living room, cathedral ceiling, wood-burning fireplace, one bedroom, unusual style. Garden, lots of plants, sounds of crickets, tree frogs, birdsong, seclusion, convenience. Perfect spot for the most creative summer of your life. Asking only, *etc., etc.*' There, doesn't that make you want to snap it up, no further questions asked?"

"What about Hugo? You don't mention him along with the birds and crickets."

Moozy didn't look pleased that I had brought up the subject. "Yes, well of course, that beast certainly *is* a problem, isn't he? A lovely animal, but it isn't a good idea to mention him in the ad, you know. First you get the client on the hook, Roger tells me, and then you let him know the drawbacks."

"Does that mean you'll be bringing people out to the house before you tell them about the dog? And then Hugo comes bounding out the door and you say, 'Oh, by the way . . .'?"

Moozy frowned and tapped on her polished desk with her polished nails. "Damn that animal. I don't suppose you could take him for the summer?"

"My mother won't allow it," I said, which was certainly true. "He's an awful lot of trouble. Sheds like anything, you know, and he sometimes forgets his manners." Which was not the truth, because Hugo is very well-behaved in all respects. His only fault is his size.

"My God," Moozy gasped. I said nothing and let her think the worst. "And the size of that animal, too."

I stared down at my thumbs and worried about what I was doing. Then I swallowed hard to get rid of my dry mouth and said, "Charlotte told you I'm sort of the caretaker while she's gone, didn't she?"

"Yes, she did tell me that, and I think it's just very, very sweet of you."

"I'm feeding and walking Hugo and doing whatever the garden needs and getting the house cleaned up for the summer tenants, before they come. If they come," I added.

"That's perfectly lovely, C.C."

"The problem is," I rattled on, before I could lose what was left of my nerve, "she forgot to leave me an extra set of keys. And she told me you have a set, so I'm wondering if you'd let me have yours. And then you can give me a call at home, or at Charlotte's, before you want to bring anybody out there, and I'll meet you."

I held my breath. It wasn't really a lie, I thought; I had given Laura the set of keys Charlotte had given me, so I didn't have an "extra" set. And this was the only way I could think of to keep her from showing up there with some clients and discovering that Laura had moved in.

"But won't that tie you down too much? Wouldn't it be better just to have duplicates made of this set? Then I wouldn't be bothering you at odd hours."

"You're right," I said, realizing that with anybody else I wouldn't have gotten even this far. "I'll have another set made and bring these back in a day or two." Promise her anything, I thought; just get the keys and worry about it later.

Moozy opened an antique cabinet hanging on the wall next to her desk and unhooked a set of keys. I could see only one other set in the cabinet. Business must have been slow. "I just have to make a notation in the file on this," she said, and that took a few more minutes of getting the file from wherever it had been put. "When did Charlotte leave?" she asked while she was writing.

"Sunday, I think."

"Sunday? And this is Tuesday? You mean Hugo's been shut up in that house for *two days?*"

"Oh, no," I said. "I've been over at least twice each day."

"But I thought you didn't have any keys," she said. Not at all suspicious; just curious. I could feel my face get hot and red. I have never been able to lie successfully in my entire life, and I certainly wasn't getting any better.

"Uhh, the back door was open. Yes. That's right. She forgot to lock it. But I don't want to leave it open. The house should be locked up."

"Oh, quite right. A safe neighborhood, but you never know."

"Yes, you never know." Sweat was running down my back, even in the air-conditioned office. Moozy asked my phone number, put the file away, and came around from behind the desk to walk me to the door.

"Can I give you a lift anywhere, love? I'm on my way to the hairdresser, and then I have a lunch date. You were lucky to catch me in."

"No thanks," I said. "I have my bike."

We walked toward a long, pale blue car parked in the Number Four space next to the house. It was the same blue as her rug, which was the same blue as her eyes.

"Isn't it sweet? I just bought it. One must keep up appearances in this game, you know. Our clients all expect us to look successful." She climbed in and swung the door shut. A window purred down automatically. "I'll be in touch," she said. The window purred back up again. She backed the huge car out of its parking place, fluttered her fingers at me, and slid away.

Not often, I hoped. But at least I had the keys.

Chapter Seven

Charlotte's driveway had become a jungle path, and hungry mosquitoes hovered in the thick, steamy air, waiting to suck my blood. At least half a dozen succeeded before I got to the house. The door was locked, and there was no sign of Laura. That surprised me, because I thought she would have been moved in and settled by then.

Inside, the house was dim and cool. Hugo yawned and rolled over. I scratched his belly and my fresh bites and wondered what had happened to my secret tenant. Somehow things felt different, but I couldn't be sure. I am not one of those people who knows instantly when a chair has been moved an eighth of an inch.

"Welcome."

Laura stepped casually out of the storage closet. I nearly jumped out of my skin.

"What are you doing in *there*?"

"That was a dress rehearsal to see how my system works. First thing I did this morning was to lay a trip wire across the driveway out near the road and to string it down to the house. It's connected to a buzzer, so when anybody drives across the wire out there, the buzzer sounds and I have about forty-five seconds to make sure I haven't left any fatal clues lying around and to get out of sight. I made it quite easily just now, but then you were riding a bike. A car would get here much faster. I read how to do it in a book. Now," she concluded, "would you like something to drink?"

We sat down at the low table in the living room and Laura served herb tea in mugs with ice cubes. I waved the keys that I had gotten from the baroness and told her that story and about how Moozy was going to call my house before she came with a prospect.

"And what if you're not at home when she calls? What if you're here?"

"Well, then I guess she comes over anyway. But I'm supposed to be here some of the time."

"What if you're somewhere else?"

"Where else would I be?"

"True."

I stopped worrying a little. The make-believe home-maker and the fake business woman then drank toasts to each other's intelligence and talent. The iced herb tea tasted smoky and awful. But I had to admit this was a good idea. Full credit to good old Laura. She had a place to live on her own, and I had the price of a bus ticket to Wisdom Peak.

"Now that you're here," Laura said, "you can answer some questions about the cleaning."

"Cleaning! You're asking the wrong person! That's one thing I am definitely not an expert on. Besides, I thought *you* were the expert."

"Even experts have certain areas of incompetence," she said, "and it takes a real expert to recognize those areas and to admit them. For instance," she went on, "I am not an expert in cleaning ovens, because I have never cleaned one. Ours was self-cleaning. I am also a non-expert in defrosting refrigerators, because ours was frost-free."

I considered reminding her that a deal was supposedly a deal, and that I would not have gotten involved in this kind of chicanery and deceit over which I was going to lose a lot of sleep if she had not promised to do the cleaning. But if she quit now, I would still have to do the cleaning, only even more of it. I had assumed that, because Laura was neat and well-organized, she was more of an expert on washing floors and windows than I was. But maybe her floor at home didn't need washing. Maybe the windows never got dirty. The possibilities were terrifyingly endless. I sighed. "Let's take a look at the oven."

It wasn't that bad. I have seen much worse, particularly the one at my house from which I had just scraped a lot of Macaroni Montage. Actually this wasn't bad at all. "In my expert opinion," I said, "you ought to forget about the oven for now. Because you'll only have to do it again later, unless you plan not to use it, either before Charlotte comes back or before a tenant moves in."

Laura looked at me disapprovingly. "That's risky. You may be a procrastinator, but I am not. I say let's do it now, really thoroughly. You can teach me how. And then I'll keep it clean as I go along. Cleaning it at the last minute in this state is just too much."

Logical, clear-headed, self-disciplined Laura. I guess we made a good balance, because I am none of these things. "You need oven cleaner to do a good job. I'll bring some from home next time," said the procrastinator.

Laura reached into her backpack and produced a spray can. "I brought a few supplies."

"Charlotte would never use an aerosol can," I said. "She probably puts a dish of ammonia in there overnight."

"Another nasty secret I'll never reveal."

Although it was not my nature or philosophy, I said, "Okay, let's get it over with." I lifted off the oven door and slid out the racks and handed them to Laura. "Spread out some newspapers," I instructed, "and put the racks on them. We'll do them last." Then I gave the can a good shake and started to spray the inside of the oven.

"According to the directions on the can," Laura said behind me, "the oven should be warm. Two hundred degrees. And you're not supposed to shake the can."

"I thought you didn't know how to clean an oven."

"I thought you *did*."

I shoved the racks back in the oven and lifted the door into place and wrestled with it until the catches caught. Then I turned the oven on to two hundred and we sat silently until the oven light clicked off and the contents of the can had settled. I went through the whole business again, taking off the door, pulling out the racks, and so on. I sprayed white foam on the sides and back of the oven. The fumes sent us both into coughing fits. There were no paper towels; my aunt does not believe in them. Laura brought me a pan of cold water and a chewed-looking sponge, and I set to work washing off the white foam that had turned brown and was running in greasy streams to the bottom of the oven.

It was going pretty well, and Laura behind me was admiring my progress. Then I noticed that a small bright bulb set in the back wall of the oven was glowing feebly through a smear of baked-on grease and flecks of dried white foam. A couple of swipes with the wet sponge would take care of that.

Pop.

Gray blistered pieces of the bulb lay scattered on the oven floor. I backed my head and shoulders out. "Rule Number One: never wash a hot light bulb with a wet sponge." I gathered the bits of glass and dumped them in the trash and finished wiping the inside of the oven. Then I reached for the racks. Still crusty, they lay on the Arts and Leisure section of *The New York Times*.

"You should have sprayed them first," Laura advised. "Now they're cooled off."

I sat back on my heels and considered the twin problems of Laura and the racks. My first impulse was to go on a spray spree, dousing everything in sight. Instead I slid the racks back into the oven, attached the door which I had also forgotten to clean, turned the oven on again (Laura began reading the Arts and Leisure section), turned it off when it was hot enough, took everything apart again, sprayed and wiped whatever needed it, and put it back together. Done.

"Now," Laura said from the high stool on which she sat swinging her legs, "what about the refrigerator?"

The sun was hanging straight overhead. All the windows in the kitchen were open, but no air moved. I wiped the sweat from my face onto the tail of my good blouse. There were greasy brown stripes on my arms and splatters on my skirt. "The refrigerator can wait."

"I think it would be a good idea to get it over with too,

while we're in the mood," Laura said, and she began in a businesslike way to take the jars and bottles and little plastic containers with dabs of food in them out of the refrigerator and line them up on the counter next to the sink. Layers of frost pushed the door of the freezer compartment partly open. "Pretty obsolete piece of machinery," she observed.

"Charlotte considers it a challenge, I believe. She says the downfall of most women is their dependency, not only on men but on modern gadgets invented by men. What she'd really like, I think, is an old-fashioned ice box. You know, the kind with a huge block of ice in it?"

"But then she'd have to depend on an ice man," Laura said, "and she'd be right back where she started from."

"She'd probably recruit one of her friends into being an ice woman. Sisterhood sticks together." I started filling pans with hot water and putting them into the freezer. Suddenly I thought of Lois, playing country lass. "Which reminds me, for no reason, how's the Shepherdess getting along?"

"Oh, fine, I guess. Somebody talked her out of getting sheep, which are very shy and delicate animals and get some horrible disease. So instead she bought a goat, and she's planning to milk her when she grows up and make cheese and so on. But goats don't eat grass, you know. They prefer shrubbery. Little Ninotchka has practically demolished Lois's landscaping. But what's really getting her down is finding out that animals are cute but that she has to get a goat-sitter while she's away on her business trips."

"Who's the goat-sitter?"

"Guess."

The refrigerator dripped. Bugs hummed. The heat pressed down. Hugo's furry bulk stretched across the door to the living room, and his tongue lolled. It was very peaceful. Then the warning buzzer sounded. I was taking a tray of melted frost out of the refrigerator. I jumped and the water sloshed, some onto the floor, most onto me.

"Somebody's coming!" I yelped. "What are we going to do with all this stuff in forty-five seconds?"

"Don't panic," Laura said calmly. "You're supposed to be here, remember? And I'm your friend here to help you out." She picked up a rag and began flicking at things on the mantle. "It's your mother's station wagon," she said. "I don't feel like answering any of her well-meaning questions, so I think I'll hide anyway. Please don't coax her to stay. I'll die in that closet."

Two car doors slammed, one right after the other, and Allison's piercing voice cut like a buzz saw through the thick air. "Anybody home?" she yelled. It was even enough to rouse Hugo from his doggy dreams. As I took a giant step over the furry mound in the doorway, the mound stretched and stood up, catching me off-balance. I pitched headlong into the living room, just as Allison jerked open the front door. "She's here," she screamed over her shoulder to my mother, who was right behind her.

"Yes, dear, I see that. Are you all right, C.C.?"

Hugo had disentangled himself from my legs and sat on his haunches, looking very dignified. I, scrambling to my feet, did not. "I'm fine. Come in, come in," I said heartily, trying to look cheerful and not as though I resented the arrival of an inspection committee.

My mother, satisfied that I had not broken any bones

or furniture, looked past me into the kitchen. "How are you doing out here?" Which translated to: *what* are you doing?

"Oh, great. I just finished cleaning the oven, and now I'm defrosting the refrigerator."

She opened the oven door and nodded approvingly, not noticing that the light bulb was missing. I can scarcely believe it," she was murmuring. "At home I can't get you to do a thing." Then she took a second look at me. "Why are you dressed like that to clean the kitchen?" I imagined that little puckers of suspicion were creeping around the corners of her mouth.

I never bother to lie, mostly because I'm so bad at it. It's much easier to tell the truth, although I sometimes re-arrange the facts, fattening in some places, thinning out a little in others. "I had to go see the woman who is in charge of renting out the house for Aunt Charlotte. And then I stopped by here to feed Hugo. And then I decided as long as I was here I might as well get some of these tough jobs done."

"I never would have believed it." She opened the door of the Meditation Room and peeked in. "What in heaven's name is *this*?" I forgot that my mother probably hadn't been in the house since Michael left and Charlotte had changed things around. So I gave her a fast explanation, hoping that Laura wouldn't sneeze or Allison wouldn't go pulling open doors the way she usually does. But Allison wasn't even there; she was poking around outside with Hugo.

"Listen, give me a chance to get the place in shape, and then I'll give you a grand tour, okay?"

"C.C., I wasn't here to check up on you. I just can't

get over any of this. Your room at home . . ." She kept shaking her head and muttering to herself about teen-age daughters who will work like slaves for other people, and so on. "Are you joining your family for dinner?" she asked in a rusty voice.

"Yes, I'll be home soon. Just a few more things to finish up here, and then I'll quit for today."

Finally she left, calling, "Come on, Allison, let's go." Allison came scrambling out of the storage shed on the far side of the garden.

The car doors slammed. Tires crunched on the gravel. Laura stumbled out of the closet. "I thought your mother had a job."

"Starts next week, I think."

"It must be a hundred and twenty in that closet," she said. "I thought they'd never go."

"Maybe you ought to find a cooler hiding place." The buzzer sounded again and I jumped. "Not another one!"

"That's just the car going out. Now the first thing we've got to do," she said, picking up and examining the little jars and containers she had taken out of the refrigerator, "is to get some decent food in here. I'm not into this vegetarian thing." She sniffed the contents of a bowl, wrinkled her nose, and set it on the floor for Hugo. Hugo sniffed it and turned away. "Neither is he," she said, and dumped the leftover soyburger into the garbage.

"You ought to try it; it's not that bad. You eat that babalooey at school all the time. At least this is good for you."

"Virtuous food, this stuff," she said. "I'd rather have it just plain awful."

By the time I had finished wiping out the inside of the

refrigerator and Laura had consigned most of the odds and ends of food to the garbage and I had mopped up all the puddles of water, it was the middle of the afternoon. I was hot and in a miserable mood, after all the work I had done, except there was a certain satisfaction in having done it. "That's enough for one day. Now what I could really use is a grape soda float with a couple of big scoops of ice cream. Strawberry ice cream."

Laura humphed. "Not likely in this house. Listen, what *are* we going to do about food?"

"*We?* What do you mean, *we?* That's your problem!"

Laura tilted her chin and looked injured. "I took it for granted you'd be eating here too, sometimes."

"Yeah, sure I will, but I can't **do** it often or my mother will know for sure something is going on. And I don't know how I can get any food for you."

"Don't worry about it. Right now it's more of a logistics problem than anything else. As long as Lois is away, I'll be all right. I have to go over there to check on Ninotchka every day, and I'll just bring food back here on my bike."

"How long will she be gone?"

"I don't know. That's another problem." She shrugged philosophically. "I'll deal with that one next. No use crossing your bridges before you come to them, et cetera," she said.

And it ended with me finally agreeing to ride with her to Lois's house in the country, miles from town with plenty of steep hills, after hours of sweaty drudgery, to check on the stupid goat and to transfer whatever food we could carry from Lois's freezer to Charlotte's. Laura got her bike out of the garden shed where she had hidden it, and we pedaled like mad out to the farm.

Laura showed me the room that was supposed to be hers: Early American with a creaky old wooden bed that looked like a sleigh, a bowl and pitcher of water on a washstand, and a braided rug. While Ninotchka danced around bleating for attention, we crammed frozen quiches and crab souffles and cream-filled Twinkies—all the things Laura considers necessary for survival—into our saddle bags and backpacks. "That should hold me for a while," she said. It looked like at least a month's supply and left quite a gap in Lois's freezer chest. "Here," Laura offered, "have a Twinkie for strength."

"Before we go," I said, "will you answer just one question? Why don't you stay *here*? I mean, you'd be alone and independent—and all the food is here already."

Laura turned on me the look she usually reserves for very small children and adults whose intelligence she thinks to be limited. "Because this is where I'm *supposed* to be. And there's no adventure in that."

We labored back to Laura's adventure and packed Charlotte's refrigerator with the fancy groceries. Laura set out one spinach-filled pastry and a fat, rigid slab labeled club steaks and another couple of packs of Twinkies. "We forgot grape soda," she wailed.

"Drink carrot juice," I suggested. "There's loads of it."

"I'll get some tomorrow," she said, ignoring my suggestion. "Can you get by with plain water tonight?"

"Hey, look, I can't eat here tonight."

"Why not?"

"Because I've been here all day, and my mother's bound to wonder what's going on. I told her I'd be home for dinner—you heard that in the closet, didn't you?"

"All right, go," she said dramatically, as though I had just doomed her to sleep alone in a snake-infested cave at the edge of a cliff.

In all the time I've known Laura, years and years it seems like, since I started getting too tall and it became evident she wasn't going to lose her baby fat, I've never seen her look so disconnected. As though the parts of her body didn't quite fit together, especially her head. She looked scared, as a matter of fact, and that puzzled me because, after all, she had gotten what she wanted. I began looking around for my shoes, which I kicked off at the door out of habit, because Charlotte never wears shoes around the house. I was stooping over to look behind the rocking chair for the one I couldn't find, and I happened to glance out of the window that faces the driveway. There, looking back in at me, grinning from one side of her face to the other and showing off the rabbit teeth that are too big for her mouth, was Allison.

"Allison!" I shrieked, squawked, groaned, all at once.

The grin disappeared from the window and reappeared at the front door.

"Allison Poindexter, what are you doing here?"

"Coming to see what you're doing."

"Nosy brat! None of your business! Anyway, you know what I'm doing here—I'm cleaning the place for Aunt Charlotte."

"What's Laura doing here?"

"Helping."

Allison flopped down comfortably on the mattresses that make a sofa bed. "Then why did she hide when I was here with Mama?" She squinted her eyes down to little slits and aimed them at Laura. "I saw your bike out in the shed, not just parked there but *hidden*. And then I found this funny wire running all the way out by the road. I figured it was some kind of a trap. So when I came back by myself I wheeled my bike through the trees. Only there was nobody here when I got here. So I was just looking around some more. Then you guys came down the drive and I heard the buzzer buzz inside the house. And I watched you unload all the food, and I looked through the window and saw you put it all in the refrigerator."

"So what?" I said in a menacing tone.

"So," said the detective, completely unrattled, "I think you're having a big party. Or something. It doesn't matter what, because I know it's something you're not supposed to be doing."

"You can't prove a thing."

"You might as well confess now," she said, "because I know how to get here anytime I want to without setting off the alarm, and I'll just spy on you until I find out, and you won't even know when I'm here and when I'm not. I'm very good at being sneaky," she said, quite pleased with herself.

I thought briefly of tearing her limb from limb. That's almost always my first impulse with Allison, who has the ability to make me madder in the shortest possible time than any other human being on the face of the earth.

"What do you want, Allison?" Laura asked very coolly, not at all upset since Allison is not her sister.

"A Twinkie for starters. Please."

Laura handed her a pack. "Have two," she said.

Allison daintily stripped off the wrapper and stuffed half the goody in her mouth. "Okay," she said, her mouth full, "now tell me what's going on here."

"And if we don't? Because you aren't going to spy on us day and night, no matter what you say. It's physically impossible."

Allison shrugged. She has very square shoulders that seem made for shrugging. "I know a lot anyway. I'll tell."

"And if we let you in on the stupendous secret?"

Allison grinned. Her grin asked to be mashed. "I'll tell anyway, unless you can persuade me not to."

"And what, darling child, can we do to persuade you to keep your sweet little mouth shut?"

She turned her squint on me. "Take me along to Wisdom Peak."

"Allison, don't be silly. You know it's impossible, because you're too young anyway, besides which I don't have enough money for both of us, and in addition I have no intention of taking along a rotten little creep—"

"Those are my terms," she announced. "Take it or leave it. Anyway I would only cost half-fare, because I'm under twelve, and I can buy my own ticket with the money I have left from Christmas and my birthday, and even enough to lend you some, if you need it." Allison knew I never could save anything.

"Allison," Laura said in a very reasonable tone that I admired, "why is it suddenly such a big thing for you to go to Wisdom Peak?"

"Lots of reasons. Because of Jennifer. I think Daddy's going to marry Libby, which will make Jennifer my sister and every time we go to see Daddy she'll be there. And what if Mama decides to marry Mr. McChesney and that Belinda dope of his is always around too?" Her face twisted into a scowl, and the scowl dissolved into tears.

"But you don't know any of these things, Allison. Do you? I mean, who told you anybody is marrying anybody?"

"Nobody." Another Allison shrug. "I just got a feeling."

"You haven't even met Belinda," I reminded her.

"I don't want to meet her. I just want us all to be the way we used to be." Her nose was running and she was snuffling. I found a wadded-up tissue in my shirt pocket. She blew.

"Wisdom Peak isn't going to do that."

She started to bawl again.

"A lot of stuff for your Family Ledger," I said to Laura.

"I gave that up," she said. After a minute she added, "The kid has a point."

We said nothing for a while. Allison subsided to an occasional sob and gasp.

"Okay," I said finally. "You win. But that trip is a long way off. Which means you've got to keep your mouth shut for almost two whole months. One slip and the deal is off, understand?"

"Right."

We shook hands, and Allison divided her second Twinkie into three parts, giving the end pieces to Laura and me and saving the creamy middle part for herself. We told Allison about how Laura was staying in Charlotte's house. She was disappointed that it wasn't something more darkly forbidden, and she wasn't quite sure she believed us. And then she and I rode home and left Laura to enjoy her first night of independence. She didn't look scared any more. I think she was glad to get rid of us.

The next morning we rode back early with Allison puffing along behind, red-faced and yelling, "Wait up! Wait up!" By the time we got there Hugo and Laura had

had their breakfasts, food and dishes were cleared away, Hugo was brushed until he looked like a model for a dog food commercial, and Laura had set up a schedule of chores.

1. Scrub and wax kitchen floor. ("Oh, *that's* how you use a waxer! Well, now I know.")

2. Launder kitchen curtains. ("This washing machine doesn't work at all like ours, and I was afraid of pushing the wrong buttons.")

3. Wash kitchen windows. ("The service that did ours always had a special rubber gadget, and I couldn't find one anywhere.")

And so on. Laura was a marvel at organizing, but it turned out that her "areas of incompetence" included most of what she liked to call technical details. The Montgomerys had always hired people who were expert at such details. In this way, Laura organized me into doing most of the heavy cleaning in about a week.

Next to organizing, Laura's big contribution was paper-sorting, which is just another kind of organizing. While I was working on the big living room window ("I can't reach the top panes, even with a ladder"), Laura sat on the living room floor in a half-lotus position (she had been reading one of Charlotte's yoga books), sorting through stacks of old *Christian Science Monitors* and *Craft Horizon* magazines and envelopes stuffed with tons of clippings and piles of paperback books and limp pamphlets about art and astrology and organic gardening and Transcendental Meditation and mind control and all the other things that Charlotte has been or is now or plans eventually to be interested and involved in. All of this had been shoved in messy heaps on the wooden boards stacked between piles of bricks along one wall. But Laura, in her new capacity as librarian, had pulled all the stuff from the shelves into one grand heap on the floor. She was planning to sort the clippings and pamphlets according to subject and put the newspapers and magazines in chronological order, and so on. The only thing wrong with this noble undertaking was that Laura is psychologically unable to pick up anything with printing on it, even to move it from one place to another, without reading it. She just can't help herself. One result of this is that it takes a long time and she doesn't get much else done. Another result is that she sometimes finds out more than she ought to.

Toward the end of the week I was sitting in Charlotte's empty bathtub in my underpants and bra, scrubbing away at the moldy stuff between the tiles with an old toothbrush. I had my tape deck for company, and I was sort of marveling at all the strange places that dirt can hide, just waiting to creep up and overwhelm you, when Laura came into the bathroom looking like she had just seen an F on her straight-A-except-for-gym report card.

"Did you know, C.C.," she asked in this high, thin voice that was not hers, "were you aware that Philip McDermott and your aunt have gone away *together* to that art colony?"

"No," I said, "I didn't know. How do *you* know?"

She waved a manila envelope at me. It had a large blue and white address label on it that I could see even from the bottom of the bathtub was from the Aberdeen Hill Colony for Writers, Artists, and Musicians. What I could not see was that the label was addressed to Mr. Philip McDermott, but Laura read me that in the same reedy voice.

Laura sat down on the bath mat and opened the envelope, which must have been opened and shut quite often because half the metal clasp was broken off and the corners were bent and fuzzy. She began pulling brochures and letters out of it, all with the same blue and white printing across the top, and arranged them along the rim of the bathtub so I could see the pictures without moving: a Victorian mansion with turrets and porches surrounded by huge trees with low-swooping branches, and then smaller pictures of little cabins among the trees, and a pond with somebody sitting next to it with an easel, and a barn with somebody looking at a huge clay head, and a silhouette through a window of somebody staring at a typewriter, and a shot of a kind of drawing room with a chandelier and a grand piano. There was also a map showing how to get there.

"Now listen to this," she said, plucking out a typewritten letter with blue and white lettering at the top. "Dated March 3rd. Addressed to Mr. Philip McDermott, 12 High Street, Greenfield. 'Dear Mr. McDermott. It is with a great deal of pleasure that we inform you of your acceptance at the Aberdeen Hill Colony. We can accommodate you from June 1st through August 15, as you requested, with the possibility of a further extension. Our Admissions Committee has been greatly impressed with *Nightmares and Nausea*, your collection of poetry, as well as with your plans for a second collection, and we hope that you will find Aberdeen Hill a good place in which to work. Please fill in the enclosed information cards and return them to us. We look forward to your arrival in June, sincerely yours, et cetera et cetera'" She put down the letter and looked at me in wounded triumph.

"It could be a coincidence," I said, not believing that it was.

Laura made a noise between a snort and a wail. "Don't

be absurd," she said, putting spaces between her words. "There's more evidence."

The evidence was a carbon copy of a letter from Charlotte Poindexter written to the colony a week later, asking to be put on the waiting list for the same period. And a letter back confirming receipt of her application and photographs of her work and letters of recommendation, including one from Mr. McDermott. And a telegram dated May 28 saying there had been a last-minute cancellation by one of the artists, and they were offering the vacancy to her. "So you see?" she said.

"Okay," I said. "But it still doesn't seem like what you think. They know each other from school, right? And he tells her about a place he's going and she says hey, that sounds interesting, maybe I could get in there too. And he says why not, give it a try, you can use my name. So they end up there *at the same time* which is not the same thing at all as going there *together*. Besides," I hurried on, "I know for a fact that she doesn't even like him because he's a male chauvinist and he probably doesn't like her because she's a radical, liberated woman and is about ten years older than he is."

"You know nothing," said Laura pityingly, stuffing letters and brochures back in the battered envelope. The other half of the clasp broke off in her fingers. "That's exactly when people get together, just when everybody else thinks they're incompatible."

This girl, my best friend and maybe even my only friend, was beginning to get on my nerves. If it were not for her, I would not be sitting in an empty bathtub in my underwear scrubbing dirt that hardly anybody—not Charlotte, probably not the tenants—would notice anyway, except a cleanliness nut. And she was bringing up subjects that I did not want to think about because I had too many other things on my mind and this was really making it overcrowded. "So what," I said, too loud, because the bathtub made it sound even louder. "That has nothing to do with us."

Laura gathered up the envelope and rushed out of the bathroom. I took about three more whacks at the mildew with the toothbrush. But I was thinking about my aunt, who was my favorite adult female, and the fact that for the past couple of years I had planned to be like Charlotte when I grew up: independent and interested in a lot of things and not afraid of Life. And now this aunt had possibly gotten involved emotionally with someone she claimed she didn't even like, and I began to see she was like all the other adults I knew who didn't know what they wanted, even when they had it. At times like this I knew that I did not want to become an adult, which was really not that much different from being a teen-ager, except that you were expected to act as though you knew at least some of the answers, and when you didn't know, you couldn't just admit it but had to fake it. I couldn't think of a single adult who wasn't faking to me about something. I cursed the mildew and my aunt and life in general and climbed out of the bathtub.

Chapter Eight

We did not let our personal feelings interfere with our work. We cleaned fanatically. We watered the garden and mowed the lawn. Laura planted some flowers. Every once in a while Baroness von Schmidt would call to say that she was bringing over a prospect. There weren't many, because most people don't want to be responsible for somebody else's gigantic dog, and Moozy had found that it was best to be honest about Hugo in the beginning. Laura didn't bother to hide any more when the buzzer sounded, because I was always there when it did and Moozy was used to seeing her with me.

Allison took charge of Hugo and kept him brushed and free of burrs. He adored the attention. Hugo had few pleasures in life. He loved to eat and he loved to sleep and he loved to have his belly scratched. He had a rubber mouse that he had stolen from a neighbor's cat, and he liked to carry that around. He was very jealous of it. A burglar could have carried off almost anything in the house without disturbing Hugo, but he guarded his rubber mouse with his life. Other dogs bored him. He wouldn't even bother to get up if one came into the yard. He disliked cats but seldom chased them and they didn't like him enough to take a chance on teasing him.

After the first few weeks we got lulled into believing that we were home free, that the property was not rentable. But one afternoon at the end of June Moozy called to say that she was on her way over with a couple of prospective tenants. She was very optimistic about them because they had once owned a kennel.

"I guess I'd better start packing," Laura said. "This sounds like the end."

We sat down in weary resignation to wait for the prospective tenants, thirty bare toes lined up on the wooden step by the front door. Allison's were decorated with splotches of bright pink polish. Hers were the dirtiest.

After a while the eye-blue Cadillac rolled down the driveway, tripping the buzzer. We didn't move. Moozy, decked out in false eyelashes even in the ninety-degree heat, got out one side while an elderly man in white shoes got out the other. He helped an elderly woman out of the back seat. She had thin wisps of bluish hair combed over her pink skull and wore very large eyeglasses. Moozy introduced us to Mr. and Mrs. Musser, who were from out of state. They told us their daughter and son-in-law lived in this town with their three lovely little boys, and rather than crowd the family by staying with them for the summer, they thought they'd find a little place of their own where they could come and go as they wanted to.

We stayed on the step while Moozy showed them through the house. It was in spotless condition, if I do say so myself. After a while they came out again, looking pleased. Moozy circled thumb and finger to show us the deal was made. Mrs. Musser thought the house was "just darlin'." Mr. Musser said, "Ho boy," to Hugo who rolled over and let his belly get vigorously rubbed. Mr. Musser walked around back to look at the garden and said it was just what he needed to keep himself busy when he wasn't playing with his grandsons. Then Mrs. Musser went around to see for herself the herb garden, which had tiny signs burned in wood to identify each specie, while Mr. Musser began the final round of negotiations with Moozy. She pulled out a lease form and a pen. Mr. Musser reached for his checkbook. It was all over.

Then Allison, who has a knack for doing the wrong thing at the right time, suddenly grabbed Hugo's rubber mouse right from under his nose and tossed it in a high arc toward the rhododendron. Hugo surged up out of his torpor and took a flying leap toward the bushes where the mouse had landed, just as Mrs. Musser came around the corner of the house carrying a sprig of mint in her hand. She had just time to say, "George . . ." when Hugo hit her head on, with a solid thump. Mrs. Musser sailed lightly, like a dandelion puff, and landed gently, still holding her sprig of mint. Her glasses dropped into the grass beside her.

For a few seconds no one moved, except Hugo, who was snuffling for his mouse among the rhododendron. Then Mrs. Musser called out, "George, help me, please." Mr. Musser went to pull her up and pick her glasses out of the grass. Moozy began to apologize in long breaths. Hugo ambled back with his mouse and lay down and closed his eyes.

Mrs. Musser squinted through her glasses and then set them back on her nose, hooking on the ear pieces. "I don't think," she said in a quavery voice, "that I could put up with that animal."

"Now, Birdie," Mr. Musser began, "he's really very gentle and friendly, long as you don't get in his way when he's movin'. Huh, boy?"

"No," Mrs. Musser said quite firmly.

Mr. Musser looked from Moozy to me and Laura and said, "We raised dachshunds." Moozy glared at me and began her sales pitch all over again. But Mrs. Musser just kept shaking her head, and after a while they all climbed back into the Cadillac. Moozy went through a number of back-and-forth maneuvers to get the car turned around in the small driveway. The windows were up because the air-conditioning was turned on, but I could see Mr. Musser waggling his fingers at us. We waggled back. Laura brought out the last of the Twinkies, and we celebrated.

A couple of days later I got a letter from Charlotte. She wrote that she was sorry we were having trouble renting the house because of Hugo, and she hoped it wasn't too much of a burden and a chore for me to keep up with everything, the garden and dog and all, for the whole summer. She said Moozy had written that I was doing a good job taking care of things. Charlotte said she really appreciated everything I was doing and her mind was at ease since I was so responsible and she was getting a lot done. She said Aberdeen Hill was a wonderful place to work and there were many stimulating and interesting people and the experience was meaningful and fulfilling.

"I can imagine what she means by *that*," Laura fumed.

"She doesn't mention Mr. McDermott," I said.

"She doesn't have to."

But there were too many other things going on for me to think much about Charlotte and Mr. McDermott.

For one thing, my mother decided to quit her job with the engineering company that she had had for less than a month and to go into business for herself. "Don't tell your father about this just yet," my mother said, as though I were in constant communication with him. "I'll tell him when the time is right."

And I found out later, my father decided to get married. "Please don't say anything at home about this," he said. "I'll tell your mother about it myself."

My mother was buying a store. It was on a side street in the middle of town, and it had been there for forty-five years as Stine's Fabrics, Inc. The show window was always covered with yellow transparent plastic to keep the sun from fading the display. Lengths of cloth pleated at one end and fanned out at the other were arranged in rays around a cardboard sun that said SAVE AT STINE'S. Every now and then somebody from the store would crawl into the window and pleat up some different fabric on the sun to show that it was a new season and time to make new clothes and then crawl out again until it was time to replace Back-to-School Corduroy with Holiday Velvet and Brocade. A narrow dingy tunnel led back from that dusty window.

When I was taking Domestic Arts in sixth grade Mr. Stine sold me some woolen braid which he claimed was cotton for a wraparound skirt and which then shrank up and puckered when I washed it and put it in the dryer. Soon after that Mr. Stine decided to retire and advertised his business for sale. But nobody would buy it, because he was asking too much for it. Then he died and his wife tried to run it, but by then everybody was shopping at a big discount fabric store in a new shopping center out on the highway. My mother had taken us out there one day the previous winter to shop for material for a new dress for Allison. "This place is ugly. Big and ugly," she said. "Who wants to buy nice things in a place like this?" Maybe that's when she got the idea of buying Mr. Stine's dingy old store and transforming it, she said later. Without telling anybody she had applied for a government loan for small businesses. She never thought she had a chance of getting it, she said, but it came through.

She had a lot of ideas for changing the image of the store. First she would completely redecorate the place, and then she'd stock it with quality merchandise and launch an advertising campaign. She planned to name it "Glad Rags."

The first thing she did was to hire Mrs. Panek, who had once owned a stationery store with her former husband and thought she knew a lot about running a business. Although my mother didn't like going to singles parties with Mrs. Panek in her slinky black dress with the silver threads running through it and sometimes said that Mrs. Panek came on a little too strong for her taste, she did admire her practical business sense.

Meanwhile, Libby was planning another of her family picnics for the Fourth of July. I could see Allison's point. About the only time we were going to see Dad was when Libby and her kids were around. We wanted to have a chance to talk to him alone, but we knew that we'd have that chance only in the car going and coming. I wouldn't have been surprised if Libby had rented a bus so that we could all travel together. Furthermore, I had a feeling that anything with Libby in charge was always a production, super-organized according to some kind of a master plan, with a theme and so on. It didn't take much to guess the Fourth of July was going to be red, white and blue and that we would probably have to eat a reconstruction of the first lunch Martha Washington served George, instead of just sitting around in the backyard and cooking hot dogs on the grill and then driving over to the park to see the fireworks and hear the band concert, like we always used to.

"Fireworks is all I care about," Allison said.

"I guess you'll get plenty of that with Libby's kids around."

We were sitting on Charlotte's wooden step, and Laura was telling us that she had seen Karen Miller the other day who told her that her parents had reconciled, which was contrary to all Laura's predictions—that Karen's father would marry his nurse and so on. "Karen said they were all very loving and too busy making up to notice that she was still going out with Sammy. They don't approve, of course."

"Why not?" Allison asked.

"Sammy's black."

"Oh," said Allison. "That's dumb."

"Karen said she didn't usually approve of the people her parents went out with when they were separated, especially the nurse in her father's office, so she didn't much care what they thought. The opinion of adults is of very little consequence," Laura told us. "We should learn not to be so influenced by it, since most of them don't know what they want anyway."

The rebellious spirit was contagious. "I'm not going on Libby's old picnic," Allison announced. "So there."

"That's a real Declaration of Independence," Laura said approvingly.

"You'll start another revolution," I warned them.

"I don't care. I'm not going, and nobody can make me."

"True. But then you won't get to see Dad at all."

"Who cares?"

We both did.

"Which side are you on?" Laura asked me. "Whig or Tory?"

"I can't remember which is which. Rebel." History wasn't my best subject.

The revolution nearly ended before it began because of dissension among the troops. Who was going to call Dad and fire the first shot? What happened finally was that I phoned Dad's office when I thought he'd be out for lunch and left a message with his secretary that sounded more like we *couldn't* go than we *wouldn't*. Then he called back and wanted to know what had happened since plans had been made for at least two weeks. I stammered around and finally told him that we wanted to see him, and we would go anywhere he wanted to go but not if Libby's kids were around. Something told me I better not include Libby herself in the ban. I admit I made it sound more like Allison's idea than mine.

"I'll think about it," he said. Later he called back again and told us he'd go to the beach during the day with Libby and her kids as originally planned, but he would come back in time to take us to the park for fireworks and ice cream.

"I'll be darned," said my mother, overhearing. "Good for you! It's that bad, is it?"

"Yes and no," I said, in the middle again.

Dad was late, which was no surprise, but only a half-hour. He drove us first to Super Cool where we ordered melted cheese and tomato sandwiches and double butterscotch sundaes, which is what we used to do on Sunday evenings before everything changed. We took the stuff with us to Wilson Park, and we found a place along the stone wall where it was cool but there weren't too many bugs. We ate our sandwiches and ice cream and tossed around Allison's old orange Frisbee. The band was playing. When it got dark the fireworks started, blooming in the sky like rare orchids. After it was over we walked slowly back to the car, letting the parking lot empty out. We were in no hurry. Allison found the Big Dipper, and Dad showed her how to locate the North Star and explained how it had always guided sailors. He liked to talk about the stars, and he was just launching into a lecture about the Pleiades when Allison yawned and her jaw creaked and we all giggled. She snuggled up against him with her arm around his waist. "This is much better," she said, "than being with all those other people."

Dad made a noise in his throat and patted his shirt pockets to find the single cigarette he had brought with him, since he was trying to quit smoking. The filter end was bent, but he straightened it and fumbled for a match. We stopped walking while he lighted it. "Maybe you should try harder to like them," he said, exhaling a long stream of smoke. "Libby and I are going to get married soon, and I'll be living with them."

"I told you so," Allison said to me.

"Told what?" Dad asked.

"That you'd be getting married soon."

"Allie, you must have known something I didn't know. We just decided a week or so ago."

"Jennifer told me a long time ago. She said her mother was working on it."

"I guess congratulations are in order," I said, to fill the gap (gasp?) that followed. "When is it going to be?"

We watched the glowing end of his cigarette move back and forth to his mouth and then shoot out over the black grass, one last Fourth of July rocket. "The end of this month," he said. Nobody responded. "I'm hoping that we'll all learn to get along with each other," he went on, "to be a real family. But I want you both to remember that you're my two best girls, and nobody is going to take your place."

The three of us walked on with our arms around each other, awkwardly because of the different heights. It felt good.

"Please don't say anything at home about this," he said. "I want to tell your mother about it myself."

"See," Allison said to me later, when we were on our way to bed. "I *told* ya."

"Right as always, Allison."

She followed me into my room, and I let her. Usually I don't, because she's a snoop and her eyes go over the room like dust rags, not missing anything.

"So what are we going to do about it?"

"About what?"

"The *wedding*, stupid!" she yelled, stamping her foot.

"Shhh! Mama isn't supposed to know yet. I guess we'll just go, that's all. We can't say we won't go to that. It's not the same as a picnic."

"That's not what I meant," she said, starting to bawl and still not being quiet. "I don't want there to be any wedding!"

I was too tired to work on this. "Oh, Allison, neither do I, but there's nothing we can do to keep them from doing what they want to do. Maybe in the end it doesn't really matter anyway, so we might just as well quit worrying."

She tripped over a throw rug heading for the door. "Okay for you," she said. "Okay. I'm going to ask Laura to help me, and Mama. They're much better at figuring out important things than you are." She banged out, slapping her feet down hard, slamming the door fiercely.

A few days later Dad phoned Mom and made an appointment to see her. They went into the room that had once been my father's home office and that my mother had converted into a sewing room after he left, but was now *her* home office. Allison and I hung around outside, hoping to overhear something but not close enough to be accused of eavesdropping, because we knew from experience that you couldn't hear anything in there anyway. You could distinguish voices, but not words, so you could tell only who was talking. First there was the low hum of my father's voice, then the higher hum, very briefly of my mother answering, then the lower hum going on and on.

Suddenly it reversed: the higher hum hummed longer, and the lower hum didn't have much chance before the higher hum was humming again. When the hums got close to the door we jumped around the corner out of sight, planning to amble out again casually so we could talk to Dad. But we heard Dad say to Mom, "Tell the kids hello for me," just as though he didn't know we were hanging around waiting to see him. We heard the screen door slam, and he was gone. We sauntered into the kitchen, pretending to be looking for something to eat but actually trying to find out how Mom was reacting to the news.

"Well, well," she said in a careful voice, as though it

might shatter. "Your father tells me he's getting married."

"He told us, too," Allison said. "How do we stop him?"

"We can't, honey. We shouldn't even think about it. The pressures of independence are just too much for some men to handle, I guess," she went on, like she was reciting from a textbook. She ran fresh water into the teakettle and put it on to boil. "I guess your father just couldn't stand all that freedom. Marriage is much more advantageous to men than it is to women, though. Men need women to take care of them more than women need men."

It was the kind of speech I heard all the time from Charlotte, but my mother had deep lines around her mouth and the ropey blue veins were standing up on the backs of her hands. You could often tell how my mother was feeling by her hands.

"Did you tell Daddy about Glad Rags?" Allison asked.

That made Mom laugh. "Yes, I did." She was measuring instant coffee into a mug that had MOTHER painted on the front of it under a picture of an old-fashioned lady with a high lacy collar and her hair piled on top of her head. "He doesn't approve. He says I'm crazy. He says good jobs are very scarce right now and I'm lucky to have one, because plenty of unqualified women—he thinks I'm an unqualified woman—are having a hard time finding a way to make a living. And he says this is no time to go into business, with the economy the way it is. He quoted the statistics for failure and asked me if I had gotten any professional advice and so on. And he told me that I know nothing about the fabric business and that I have never worked in any kind of store and don't know anything about the retail business. He says I should work for a couple of years for a fabric store before I try to have one on my own. And he says it's especially dangerous to try to take over somebody's failing business, that I should have tried to find one that was on the way up, not on the way down. He also thinks competition from Fabric World out on Route 1 will kill me. Other than that, he couldn't find anything wrong with the idea."

The tea kettle whistled. Mom poured the water into her mug and added milk and sugar.

"What did you say to all of that?"

She shrugged, stirred, and took one hot sip. "Not much. I just reminded him that he hadn't known a whole lot more about the laundry supply business when he started that."

"What did he say then?"

"He said that was different."

"Why?"

"Because he's a man."

"Did he really say that?"

"Oh, he said times were different, he was much younger, he had experience, and so on. But that was what he *meant*." She winked at me over her cup of steaming coffee. I saw that her hands were calm again. "Maybe," she said, "we should say a short prayer for the future Mrs. Poindexter. She's going to need all the help she can get."

Later Allison said to me, "She's not going to try to stop the wedding either." Everyone was letting her down.

"Listen, Allie," I said, "everything changes, whether you want it to or not. Everything. Even if the thing you want doesn't exactly happen the way you want it to, something else will happen and that will make the first thing different anyway. Do you understand?"

"No."

"Okay, try it this way. The main reason you don't want them to get married is because you can't stand Jennifer and the rest on family picnics, right?"

"And Christmas," she added. "Have you thought about what Christmas is going to be like?"

I hadn't, and I didn't want to. "By then it might be different. And we don't have to go. We can refuse, just like the Fourth of July picnic. And maybe in a year or so Jennifer will be an entirely different kind of kid, and you'll be best friends."

"Never. I'd rather die."

I gave up for the time being. I knew how she felt.

Then Libby phoned. She said it was Elizabeth Haas calling. I didn't recognize the name or the voice. I thought it was someone for my mother. "No, no," the woman said, "it's *Libby*—your father's, ahh, fiancee."

One of life's embarrassing moments. I apologized.

"What I'm calling about is to ask you to be in the wedding. You and Allison. Jack and I want all the children as our witnesses. I hope it's something you'll want to do, too?" She made it a question.

It wasn't, but I said yes anyway and felt like a traitor. Then I handed the phone to Allison, explaining who it was, and after a while Allison said yes, too. When she hung up, we didn't look at each other right away. Then she said, "Libby thinks it would be cute if we both wore the same dress at the wedding."

"You and I? The same dress? That would look pretty funny. You in the top half and me in the bottom or the other way around?"

It took a few seconds for my joke to sink in. Allison

never seemed to appreciate my sense of humor, but this time she laughed and socked me hard on the knee. "*Matching* dresses, dumbhead. Like twins. And not you and me— me and Jennifer."

"That sounds like fun."

"Maybe to you it does. Not to me. Do you think Libby will wear a long white dress and a veil and all?"

"I doubt it."

"It doesn't sound like a very good wedding." She picked at the hard skin around the thumb she used to suck. "I can't find the album," she said. "I looked all over."

I knew the album she meant, and I hadn't seen it either. It was a white leather book with OUR WEDDING stamped on the front in gold letters, and underneath that JOHN AND MARGARET POINDEXTER and the date. It used to be kept on the bottom shelf of a night stand on Mom's side of the double bed. When I was younger and Allison was still tiny and fairly easy to entertain, we used to creep quietly into our parents' room and get out the album and sit curled in the snug valley between the bed and the radiator with the window above it. We held the album like a sacred book, a Bible, turning the plastic-covered pages and staring at the pictures of those strange people who were our mother and father.

It seemed important to find the album, but I didn't want to ask my mother where she had put it. I spent a long time searching for it, and I finally found it in the blanket chest in the hall, all the way at the bottom, beneath a lot of wool sweaters. I looked through it again and then put it back in the chest, on top of everything so Allison could find it if she wanted to.

The main picture was a portrait of my mother in a shimmery white dress with long tight sleeves. The skirt was very full and much longer in the back than in the front. That back part was swirled around in front of her, like a pool at her feet, and the photograph was lighted so that the veil seemed to float around her head. She held a bouquet of white roses arranged in a cascade in front of her like a shield. In the next picture my father stood beside her, looking as though his suit was cut out of one piece of metal and bent around him. His hair was very short and started high above his ears. A smaller version of that picture in a silver frame used to stand on my mother's dresser and was the first thing to disappear after my father left.

Then came a group picture with all the bridesmaids and ushers. The bridesmaids wore matching dresses and hats. The maid of honor—Charlotte—matched the rest of them, except for color. Her dress was darker than theirs.

The other pictures in the album showed different scenes from before and after the wedding. I couldn't imagine why anybody had bothered to take them. For instance, there was one of my mother looking at herself in the mirror while Charlotte, who had curled hair and wore a little hat covered with artificial flowers, was fussing with her veil, and they were smiling at each other's reflection. Our two grandmothers, one wiry and very strong-looking with a tight, fierce mouth and the other fat with a few chins and a soft look as though the stuffing had started to leak out of her, stared straight at the camera. In between them was my grandfather who had died a few years ago, a gentle man with a solemn look for the occasion. You couldn't tell from the photograph which of the grandmothers he belonged to. The flash reflected blankly on three sets of eyeglasses. Another picture showed him with my mother. She was holding onto his arm, and he was kissing her awkwardly on the cheek as though she was a stranger selling kisses at a carnival booth.

There was a shot of my father and Uncle Ted, who hadn't married Charlotte yet, holding champagne glasses. The bride and groom kneeling in front of the minister; from the back you couldn't tell who they were—just a man in a metal suit and a cloud of white veil. A close-up of a man putting a plain gold ring on a woman's finger. (The ring was in my mother's jewelry box; sometimes she rubbed the spot on her finger where it used to be.) A picture of my mother throwing her bouquet right at Charlotte, and another one sliding a fancy garter over her knee. Cutting a slice of wedding cake, both my mother and father holding the knife. Mom and Dad running down the steps of the stone church with confetti swirling around them. The two of them in the back seat of a car, smiling matching smiles. The last picture was the back of the car with a JUST MAR-RIED sign on it and their profiles outlined in the rear window as though they were about to kiss. That was the end of the book. There were a few loose snapshots stuck in the back, taken on their honeymoon in Bermuda.

"Where was I?" Allison demanded each time we looked through it, and logical explanations didn't satisfy her. Something important had happened without her. It took years for Allison to get over being insulted because she wasn't there. Every time we looked at them she studied each photograph for some glimpse of herself, and I tried to explain that this had all happened eight years before she was born. "I wasn't there either," I consoled her. "It was even three years before I was born."

"Did your parents go through all that nonsense?" I

asked Laura later. She was fussing with the petunias she had planted around Charlotte's front steps, and I was flopped on the grass watching.

"Hell, yes," she said. "At St. Bartholomew's on Park Avenue, my dear, with the reception at the Colony. Ridiculous."

"How many bridesmaids?"

"Ten. And a ring bearer and flower girl. How about yours?"

"Six, plus the maid of honor. Charlotte. The reception was at the country club. We're just simple folk."

Laura put down the little fork she was using to scratch around the petunias and sat down beside me. "Be interesting to see what they go in for the second time," she said. "What are your dad and Libby cooking up?"

"I don't know the details, but Libby wants Allison and Jennifer to dress alike."

"Christ," Laura said. Lately Laura had been swearing a lot. I took it as a sign of her new independence.

We lay on our backs in the shadow of the house and watched some cream-puff clouds move majestically across the sky.

"What's your wedding going to be like?" I asked her. "When you find your interdependent relationship."

"Funny you should ask," she said. "I was thinking about that recently." There was hardly anything Laura hadn't thought about. "You know Lois was married in her mother's wedding gown, and my grandmother has been preserving it for me? It's vacuum-packed in some kind of time capsule so the polluted air won't rot it. But she had a twenty-one inch waistline. Twenty-one inches! Can't you see me cramming myself into it? So I thought I'd slit it up both sides and wear jeans and just stick my head up through all the satin and lace and seed pearls and let it all sort of waft around me. Doesn't that sound cool—jeans and sneakers and a 1932 wedding dress? And then I thought we'd have the ceremony someplace exotic, like Machu Picchu, or Katmandu, or Disneyland. Depending on my partner and what kind of work we're doing. What about you?"

I studied the cream-puff clouds and tried to dream up something half as interesting as Laura's. She could out-fantasize me any time. For instance, she would never have looked at those clouds and thought of anything so ordinary as cream puffs. To her they would be some rare flower or extinct animal.

"The Islands of Langerhans," I said, grabbing feebly for something different. I had heard of them somewhere, and the name sounded romantic. "How about getting married there?"

Laura hooted and rolled over on her side. "You're too much!"

"What's so hilarious?"

"Asshole!" (There she went again.) "Don't you really know? The Islands of Langerhans are little thingies in your pancreas. They produce insulin in your *body*."

Oh-oh. But I recovered fast. "So then I could honeymoon with a cruise through the alimentary canal."

"That's an old joke."

"Okay."

Silence for a few minutes. I thought about weddings. The cloud changed into a chicken.

"Do you think your mother was a virgin when she got married?" Laura's question.

"Yes." But I wasn't sure.

"Did she tell you she was?"

"Not in so many words. But she keeps saying things were a lot different when she was young, and that she hardly knows what she ought to be telling me. Her mother used to lecture her on purity. Virginity was sort of a precious gem that had to be fiercely protected until you were safely married. She says I'd just laugh at her if she told me that now. But I have a feeling she still thinks it's a gem. Maybe only semi-precious."

"You mean a garnet? That's closest to a cherry, right?"

"You—are—too—much!" I couldn't remember that we had ever had such a raunchy conversation.

"Lois keeps asking me if I'm a virgin. Like she used to ask me if I had gotten my period."

"What do you tell her?" I knew yes was too simple an answer for Laura.

"I tell her I have no sexual needs."

"What the hell does that mean?"

She sat up and looked at me. "That there's nothing a male can do for me that I can't do for myself." She crawled back to her petunias, and I studied the piece of information I had never dared ask anybody.

"Maybe I'll be living in a commune," I said, to get to a safer subject, "and we'll just get married there. Guitar music and everybody singing and all. And we'll all get dressed up in stuff from Community Clothes." I pictured myself decked out in a flouncy dress and shawl and floppy hat, holding hands with a tall, shadowy figure in unmatched socks. I waited for Laura to steer the conversation back to sex, because there were things I needed to know. But she was whistling around her petunias, and I'm not much for asking tough questions.

Chapter Nine

Hand-lettered invitations to the wedding on July 29 arrived in the mail two weeks before, one for Allison, one for me. With mine was a note, not in my father's writing: "Dinner in honor of the sixteenth birthday of C.C. Poindexter, July 24. R.S.V.P."

My birthday was not until August fourteenth, but on that day they would still be in Nova Scotia on their honeymoon.

There was another reason for celebrating my birthday three weeks early, it turned out, instead of a couple of days late. Dad made a little ceremony of presenting me with a gift, a square box wrapped in paper with pretty-faced teenagers sipping sodas and playing tennis and riding bicycles all over it. I wound up the thick pink yarn and peeled the paper off carefully, in case anybody wanted to use them again. Inside was an Instamatic camera with a card saying "From Dad and Libby with lots of love," in the same writing as the invitation. There were also three packages of film and three of flash cubes, each wrapped in the fancy paper and tagged "from Scott," "from Billy," and "from Jennifer." Who weren't there at the dinner. "Thank God," Allison muttered when she saw we were alone except for Libby.

"Hey, this is really terrific," I said. "I've been dying for a camera." That was the truth, but what I was dying for was a camera like Dad's, a single-lens reflex with a light meter built into the lens. Of course I didn't say that. I held the little Instamatic up to my face and squinted through the viewfinder so they couldn't see any sign of disappointment.

"The idea," Dad said, "is that we'd like you to take pictures at the wedding reception. That's why we're giving it to you now."

"I better practice," I said, and I loaded the film and stuck on the flashcube. Then I snapped pictures of Libby putting the birthday dinner on the card table. The theme was Italian that night, which was fine with me. There were dripping candles stuck in straw-covered wine bottles, red tablecloth, white plates, green napkins—the colors of the Italian flag, as Libby pointed out. The antipasto looked as though it should have been in a magazine, so naturally I took a picture of that, and of Dad pouring wine into their glasses after he had filled ours with fruit drink.

It was very hot in the apartment. Dad's air-conditioner rumbled loud enough to drown out the conversation, but the feeble waves of coolness it produced never reached us around the crowded card table. Dad sagged limply in his canvas chair. "Only one more week in this place. Libby's air-conditioners work better than mine, which is the main reason I'm marrying her." He reached for her hand and squeezed it. She smiled serenely. She didn't look as though the heat bothered her at all.

Allison expertly served herself all the hard-boiled eggs with anchovies on the antipasto platter and would have taken most of the provolone if I hadn't managed to get some first. She later proceeded to dismantle the lasagne so that she avoided the layers of ricotta cheese. Nobody tried to get her to eat anything she didn't want, and it was a peaceful meal.

I got my camera again when the birthday cake appeared. Libby apologized about seven times for resorting to a store-bought cake instead of making the Sicilian cassata she had originally planned. She said she was busy finishing a manuscript for a new book so that she could go to Nova Scotia with a free mind. And there were all the wedding details to attend to. I have no objection to bakery cakes. They're always very sweet. This one had pale green icing swagged around the sides and HAPPY BIRTHDAY c c squirted next to a bunch of yellow roses that had gotten flattened on the way from the bake shop. My father took a picture of me with the cake, and Libby took one of Dad and Allison and me. Then we ate the cake with some pistachio ice cream and the party was over and Dad drove us home again.

"I'll see you next Saturday," he said. The day of the wedding. "I'll pick you up about three. You kids know what you're supposed to wear and all?"

"Yuh," Allison answered for both of us.

I hadn't thought about *Mr.* Haas until we went to Libby's house on the day of the wedding. Nobody ever talked about her ex-husband, but I realized suddenly as we walked up the driveway that he must exist somewhere. He had once been Libby's husband, and I knew that he was the kids' father—that's usually where they were when they weren't with Libby. I didn't know his first name or where he lived now or anything about him, but I wondered about him when I went up the steps of the house where he used to live, a big white place with porches all around it and a turret on the second floor and stained glass trim on the doors and windows. I wondered if he had painted all the porch railings and mowed the grass and clipped the bushes. How would he feel when he came back to pick up his kids and saw this other man, my father, sitting on his porch with his feet up on the railing and a can of beer in his hand? I didn't know how my father felt when he came to see us. Did he miss us, the house, my mother, any of his old life? He had a whole new life—new home, new mate, everything different. Even new children, no matter what he said. But we had the same old life with a big hunk of it missing. For a minute I got so mad at him, so furious at all of them, that I wanted to scream: "Selfish bastards, all of you! You don't care what happens to *us!*" and run away and never lay eyes on any of them again. Then I thought about Wisdom Peak and how nice that would be, and that calmed me down again. The hell with all of them. Everything always changes anyway.

The ceremony took place under a mammoth tree in Mr. Haas's front yard. The people all parked their cars in the empty lot across the street. Libby had hired some kid to show them where to park. Then people gathered in whatever spots of shade they could find near the main tree and stood around complaining that this had to be the hottest day of the year. At four o'clock the stereo, concealed in some bushes next to the house, blasted out some trumpet music, and Libby walked out of her front door in a long yellow dress trimmed with white lace, like a Victorian valentine. She carried a little bouquet—a nosegay, she called it—and she paused on the top step and smiled at my father who waited at the bottom. He held out his hand and she came down the steps to him. Then they walked together to the tree. He held her elbow as if he was afraid she might trip and fall and shatter. I don't think Libby is the kind of person who ever trips, let alone shatters. The rest of us—the five kids—also waited at the bottom of the steps and trooped along behind them. Libby had given up the idea of having Jennifer and Allison dressed alike, so they each wore party dresses and had identical bands of daisies in their hair and looked unnaturally sweet. I wore a long skirt made quickly from some seersucker left over from Mr. Stine's stock that Mom and Mrs. Panek were trying to get rid of, and one of my mother's blouses which was a little tight across the shoulders. I hoped it wouldn't rip. We carried bunches of daisies that wilted in our hands. Scott and Billy were all dressed up, too, Billy looking scared and unhappy, Scott with his mouth twisted in a sour, knowing smile.

A friend of Libby's performed the ceremony, which they had made up with quotes from their favorite writers, and the music on the stereo was supposed to match up with the different words of the ceremony. But another friend who was supposed to be following the script got confused, and the Beatles came bursting out once when it was supposed to be Henry Purcell. I don't think anybody noticed the three-century gap, but that's the kind of thing that can really rattle Libby.

My father put a heavy gold band on Libby's hand, and then she put one like it on his. Dad never wore a ring when he was married to my mother. He always said he didn't like rings, that they annoyed him. But as I kept trying to tell Allison, things do change.

After the ceremony there was a lot of hugging and kissing and laughing. Everybody seemed so happy. I wanted to be happy, too, but the big hollow ball inside me would not let me, and I just hoped that I wouldn't make a complete fool of myself and cry.

Libby and Dad led the way back up to the porch, where food was spread out on long tables. The tables were all covered with yellow cloths. I counted six different kinds of cheese, four kinds of salad, a huge ham with a criss-crossed crust of brown sugar and cloves, and a turkey that had been completely sliced and then put back together again so that it appeared to be whole and uncut until you looked closely. There were roses carved out of radishes, and carrot curls, and stuffed tomatoes, and each deviled egg was decorated with a flower made out of pimiento with bits of chive for stems. "It's just too gorgeous-looking to *eat*," a woman gurgled.

Then I heard a man say, "Well, Mrs. Poindexter, did you make all of this beautiful food yourself?"

That was when it finally hit me that her name was now Poindexter, the same as mine. I loaded a plate with food I didn't want and hunted for a place to sit where I could watch without being watched. There weren't many choices. Finally I picked a spot on the grass near some bushes and eased myself in among the low-hanging branches.

The woman who was helping with the serving and cleaning up came out of the kitchen with a large tray and began to fill in the gaps on the decorated platters where people had taken away food. The idea seemed to be that it was never supposed to look as though anybody had eaten anything. My father was fixing himself a ham sandwich, dabbing mustard from a fancy, old-fashioned, silver pot, and the woman with the tray stopped to speak to him. I couldn't hear what she said. I don't know why, but the woman made me think of my mother, although she didn't look at all like her. Maybe it was the way she moved.

Then in that peculiar way my mind has, I saw this movie running behind my eyeballs, a movie in which instead of the maid it was my mother carrying those plates of food and my father saying to her, as though he had never seen her before in his entire life, that she certainly had done a very nice job with the arranging. As though he were an enchanted prince who didn't recognize anybody. And my mother was smiling in a friendly polite way, because she knew there was something in the food, the mustard or maybe the stuffed tomatoes, but just the ones she made sure he and Libby ate, that would make them violently ill. The film kept on running in my head: my mother would have the antidote, which she would give at first only to my father and then, because my mother is a very good person, she would give some to Libby too, and she would nurse them until they were recovered. And my father's enchantment would be broken and he would be so touched by my mother's compassion and tenderness that he would insist upon marrying her instead. Libby would understand, seeing that of course he belonged with his rightful wife and children. Maybe she would even go back to Mr. Haas. Then I would snap photographs of my parents' wedding, making sure this time that Allison was in them.

At that moment I remembered that I had left my Instamatic camera inside Libby's house, and that I had not yet taken a single picture. The house was cool and darkly quiet. I wondered why everybody stayed outside in the heat when they could be in here. Probably because the bar had been set up outside, on the porch. The only inside activity seemed to be in the kitchen, where the maid and the bartender went in and out, and somebody was washing dishes and glasses.

I picked up my camera from the end table next to the fancy sofa—another Victorian valentine in carved wood and velvet—and started to go back outside. But on second thought I decided to stop in the bathroom first, under the stairs in the hall. The door was locked, and when I rattled the knob, Allison's voice croaked from within, "Go away!"

"Allison? Will you be out soon?"

"No! Go away!"

"Are you okay?"

"No! I'm sick! Go away!" Sound of throwing up.

I went upstairs, feeling like a trespasser but glad to be away from all the people. Several rooms opened off the big hall. One was yellow and flouncy, a mother's idea of how a little girl's room should be decorated. The next was plain and neat and nearly bare, except for animal posters on the walls. Billy's, probably. Then one painted in awful garish colors—kind of a Day-Glo orange with green trim. There were pictures of unlikely-looking racing cars pasted on the ceiling, partly assembled (or disassembled) plastic models scattered on the floor, the desk, the shelves, along with magazines, records, and clothes. Junk everywhere: a mess. Not much different from my room, really, except that it was male mess.

I found the bathroom next. It had a window looking down on the lawn, would in fact have been a great place for watching the wedding. Not bad for taking pictures, either, except for the screen in the window. My father was going around with a champagne bottle, refilling everyone's glass. Libby was following him, gesturing toward the porch and the food, urging everybody to eat.

I should have gone downstairs right then. There was no reason to stay upstairs in that strange house, except for my own nosiness. The only closed door led into the turret room. I couldn't resist. I peeked in; it was Libby's study. The curving walls were solidly lined with books, and her huge desk was covered, except for one small polished space in the middle, with orderly stacks of papers. Jackets from her books were framed and hung next to the windows. The room seemed to be as well-organized and serene as Libby herself. I closed the door carefully.

That left the master bedroom. It was purple. Purple with lots of mirrors and a thick white furry cover on the king-size bed. This didn't seem like Libby. There were open suitcases on a bench by the window. I recognized my father's shirt in one of them. His jacket was hung over the open lid of the suitcase. An ashtray with one butt on the bedside table. Dad's; Libby doesn't smoke, and he was still trying to quit. There was a little bathroom next to the bedroom. I opened the medicine chest and catalogued the usual stuff: aspirin, a few bottles with Elizabeth Haas, take one three times daily, typed on the label. Razor, blades, shaving cream. Dad's, or for Libby's legs? I went back to the bedroom and opened a closet door. Her stuff, his stuff. All moved in, everything settled.

I looked again at the fur-covered bed. Mr. Haas's bed, now my father's and hers. Didn't they feel *funny* about that? I wondered if Dad ever spent the whole night here, when the children were with Mr. Haas. How long had they known each other before they got into this bed together, or into his water bed at the apartment? (The water bed! What had he done with it? Maybe he gave it to Mr. Haas, in exchange for this king-size bed, wife thrown in, no extra charge.) My mother and Mr. McChesney? Did they? Her bed or his? Was I ever in the house, upstairs in my room, Allison and me asleep, not knowing, while downstairs in my parents' double bed—Martha Washington tufted heirloom bedspread, non-allergenic pillows—they did it, too? Making love, my mother called it. And then did she tell him to leave before daylight, sneak out and coast the car silently down the driveway so we wouldn't wake up and be shocked?

"I have to *go*," whined a voice behind me, surprising me so that I practically fell on the king-size bed, "but your sister won't get out of the downstairs bathroom."

"Why don't you use the other upstairs bathroom, Jennifer?"

"Because my brothers use it. They're pigs. I won't touch anything they use. They pee all over the seat. So I always use my mother's bathroom. She lets me."

I wondered how my father was going to feel about that. While Jennifer used that facility, I hurried down to see what was happening to Allison, but the downstairs john was empty and Allison was nowhere in sight.

"Have some champagne," said my father when I went outside again. He offered me a glass with bubbles clambering madly up through the hollow stem.

"No thanks," I said. "I don't think I'd like it. I don't like anything alcoholic."

"This is different," he insisted. "Try it and see. Anyway, I want my beautiful daughter to drink a toast on her old man's wedding day."

Old man? He didn't look like an old man, even though he was forty-five. He had taken up jogging and lost some weight, and his chest didn't slant out toward his belt buckle the way his friends' do. He was very proud of this, and he had some new clothes to show off what good condition he was in. Instead of the one-piece metal suit he wore in the pictures in the old wedding album, he was dressed up in a close-fitting western shirt with hip-hugger pants and a cotton handkerchief around his neck. He let his hair grow down to his collar and had it styled. I thought he looked much better than the younger man in the old picture with the hair that started so high above his ears.

I took the glass of champagne and sipped some. Actually it wasn't too bad, although it wasn't that good either. I carried the glass around with me while Dad introduced me to some of his friends. I always hated that business of meeting people, which is partly because I'm so tall and always feel like everyone is staring at me. My mother says I will get over being shy about it when I am older and less self-conscious. But I will still be taller than practically everybody else when I am older. It's not like bad skin, which can get better, or fat, which you can lose. If you're small for your age you can at least have the hope of growing. But there's no hope for getting over being tall.

I sipped on the champagne and didn't mind so much being stared at. Maybe they weren't even staring. They didn't seem especially interested in me. They kept telling Dad how great he looked, and he kept saying it was all Libby's doing, that she had made him get into shape. Then they all said she looked marvelous too, and what a wonderful couple they made. I wondered if they would have said the same thing about my mother. Finally when Dad got involved in a conversation that I didn't know anything about, I wandered away by myself, carrying the glass in one hand and my camera that I still hadn't used in the other. The bartender filled my glass for me again—was that my third?—and I decided to go take a look at the wedding cake and maybe do a nice portrait of it.

The cake was three-tiered with fluted Greek columns holding up each tier, all three draped and swagged with ribbons of icing. A ring of real yellow and white daisies circled the bottom of each layer. A miniature bride and groom stood on top, and by damn if that tiny doll wasn't wearing a yellow dress trimmed in bits of lace. Too much! A big fly, black and rainbow-shiny as oil slick, buzzed around it, bumping clumsily up against the silky white icing. Finally it sat down, right on one of the ribbons, and started crawling along. I watched him. He didn't belong there. He was dirty, and I certainly couldn't take a picture of a wedding cake with a big black fly on it. I swatted at him, just enough to shoo him away. He flew, and my thumb jabbed into the middle tier. I pulled it out and sucked off the icing. Big hole there. Yellow crumbs spilled out, like stuffing from a pillow. When I tried to patch it, it looked worse. Best thing, I thought, was to turn it around so the hole wouldn't show. By the time I got it moved, there were a few more smudges in the icing, and the bride and groom on top were facing the wrong way. Lucky for me, I knew, that everybody was still drinking out on the lawn.

Not everybody. Scott was leering at me. "You're loaded," he said.

"You're out of your mind." Note the quick retort.

"Little Allison is puking her brains out all over the bathroom and Big C.C. is drunk. Fantastic! What kind of a family has Mother Elizabeth married into anyway?"

"A very distinguished one," I said with enormous dignity, which is not easy when your tongue feels fat.

He stared at me as though he was trying to x-ray my brain. Really not a bad looking kid, this Scott, A strong build, maybe as tall as I am when he's done growing: thick hands with bitten nails, brown eyes; pale skin with hardly any pimples but a lot of small scars; peach-colored hair, sort of pale reddish-gold, wavy. Clean, too. I thought of touching it. "Want to turn on?" he asked softly.

Oh wondrous day! Everybody I knew smoked marijuana sometime or other, except Laura, I guess. And except me. Lack of opportunity. Again. The story of my life, but maybe a new chapter was going to be written. So back up the oaken staircase I went, very carefully, following this kid with the beautiful hair. But by the time I reached the top step I was already wondering if I really wanted this new chapter.

"Make yourself at home," he said.

I dug out a space on the messy floor and sat down, using his bed as a backrest, while Scott gouged around in an overflowing drawer and pulled out a Noxema jar. I watched him juggle the cigarette papers and the gray-green grass and very deftly produce a tiny white tube with the ends twisted shut. He lit it, dragged on it so hard I thought he was going to swallow it, and handed it to me.

Oh fine, I thought; what now? However: with a little flourish I put it between my lips and, faking it, sucked, trying to look as though I did it every day of my life.

"What's the matter with you?" Scott demanded. "Don't tell me this is your *first time?* God!" He smacked his forehead and groaned.

I passed him the little tube and wished I was outside not knowing what to do with champagne instead of up there with him not knowing what to do with that pot. And then I decided to hell with it, I wasn't going to smoke it, and if he thought I was weird or something that was his problem. "Listen, you just go ahead and finish it yourself," I said generously. "I'm probably not in the mood or something." Definitely "or something."

"I don't believe it, I just don't believe it," he kept muttering. "You go to Greenfield High, right? Man, I thought everybody there was stoned all the time!" He drew the smoke into his lungs and held it until I thought he must be going to pass out and then let it trickle out his nostrils. "Listen, I bet I know what you'd like," he announced, looking all-knowing and crawling over to his desk. From the depths of a jumbled drawer he pulled out a bottle of red wine and a muddy-looking glass, obviously often used and seldom washed. He filled the glass and handed it to me. "More your style," he said.

I thanked him graciously and sipped at it.

After a while Scott said, "Do you realize that you and I are now *related?* I mean, that you're my fuckin' *sister* or something?"

175

Somehow it seemed awfully funny at the time. We laughed a lot and wondered if we were half, or step, or what. I was feeling very relaxed. "You got nice hair for a brother," I said, still wanting to touch that shining goldish stuff.

"You got nice tits for a sister," he said, and I could feel my skin prickle as he stared.

I said thank you—what else is there to say?—and folded my arms over my chest, unfolding the right arm once in a while to raise the wine glass. I wondered if he'd notice I was faking that, too. After what seemed a long time, I pushed the glass (still full) under his bed. Then I concentrated on standing up, carefully rearranging my legs for balance and leverage and so on. "I think I'd better go downstairs and see what the bride and groom are up to," I said. "You coming?"

"Huh-uh. You know, your ass isn't bad either."

Tits! Ass! Something besides height! He was smiling at me, and I noticed he wasn't sneering for a change. I also noticed for the first time that he wore braces on his teeth. I stared at his mouth, but when it moved to say something else I began a slow rotation and navigation toward the door and vanished from his gaze.

The wedding reception was still going on. What can I say about it? I wanted it to be over, and eventually it was. The eating and drinking and talking and laughing ended. None of it had anything to do with me. I had a large, swollen feeling in my head and still carried the camera, loaded with film and set to go. Dad came and said they were ready to leave, they'd drive us home. Allison was already in the back seat, looking pale and wrung out, rolled in the corner like a poisoned spider. Libby came out of the house dressed in jeans and a plaid shirt for the trip to Nova Scotia. Rock music thudded from Scott's window. Billy sat on the steps, his hands hanging loose between his knees, an orphaned look on his face. Jennifer danced around Libby, clinging to her, begging promises of gifts to be brought back for her. Libby instructed them to be perfect angels until their father came for them. The phantom Mr. Haas. At last we drove away.

My mother was in our driveway, dragging bolts of cloth out of the back of the station wagon, which now had a sign painted on the side, GLAD RAGS. A lot of Mr. Stine's ancient stock of fabric didn't suit my mother's idea of what her customers would want, and she had decided to store it in our garage until she could sell it off bit by bit on special. When she heard Dad's car she leaned against the tailgate and waited for us to drive up. She had a kind of amused smile on her face, as though she knew a joke and wasn't going to share it.

"Reception committee," Dad muttered.

Libby said nothing. She scrunched forward, practically under the dashboard, so Allison and I could crawl out of the tiny back seat. She obviously didn't want to confront my mother, but Mom wasn't going to let the moment pass. She walked over and reached for Libby's hand. "My best wishes for you both," she said. "I know you'll be very happy."

Libby said thank you, sounding a little shy and embarrassed, and then my mother went around to the other side of the car where my father still sat behind the wheel, and she leaned through his open window and kissed him on the cheek, as though they were old acquaintances but not close friends. Now that would make a picture for a wedding album, I thought. "The best in the world, Jack," she said. Then she waved cheerily and went into the house. My mother was wearing jeans, too. She looked better in them than Libby did. I wondered if my father noticed that.

"Have a good trip," I said, since I had to say something. I felt like crying again. My father must have noticed, because he got out of the car suddenly and put his arm around me.

"Have a good birthday," he said, hugging me. "Maybe we'll celebrate again when I get back."

"Thanks. But once is really enough. It was terrific, really."

"It's going to be a terrific year," he said, and then he kissed Allison and got back into the car with his new wife and they drove away.

I hadn't taken a single picture of them.

Chapter Ten

On the morning of the Grand Opening—three days after my father's wedding, two weeks before my sixteenth birthday, 379 days before I could go to live at Wisdom Peak with parental permission, two weeks and two years without it—I was balanced on a ladder, doing my part to transform Stine's Fabrics into Glad Rags, Inc. Mrs. Panek had already threatened to quit at least twice.

As soon as the word got around that my mother was opening a store, everybody started giving her advice. First there was my father, who was opposed to the whole idea, but since he was in Nova Scotia on a honeymoon, his opinion didn't really count. Fred Montgomery, the Curator, gave advice, too, but Mom was paying for that. Lois, who usually handled interior design, was taking a boat trip down the Snake River in hopes of meeting an athletic, outdoorsy man, and Fred told Mom she could either hire him to do the whole job of redecorating the store, or she could hire him on an hourly basis as a consultant. She decided she could afford him for exactly two hours. For that she got advice on how to move the counters around, what color to paint everything (white with orange trim) and what lights to install for dramatic effect. The first two ideas she didn't like and the third was beyond her budget.

Then there was Alex McChesney, the Australian beagle who had been taking my mother out for dinner and movies and whatever else adults do for entertainment two or three times a week. He was the business editor of *The Greenfield Sentinel*, and he wanted to set up an advertising campaign for Glad Rags. Big ads every night for a week, announcing the Grand Opening, and then small ads after that every day with big ones only near the weekend. But that cost a whole lot, too, and besides it wasn't what my mother had in mind. She said she wasn't interested in mass appeal and—with all due respect to Mr. McChesney—most of the *Sentinel* readers wouldn't be her customers anyway. Her idea was to mail pamphlets to the people she thought *might* be customers—women with money who weren't attracted by the low, low factory-to-you prices of Fabric World out on Route 1.

Mr. McChesney said that was the height of impracticality, probably wouldn't work, and was going to be as expensive as newspaper advertising.

Not if you do most of the work yourself, my mother told him. Not if you put together an actual collection of swatches and make sure they get to the right people.

He said the whole idea was amateurish.

"Really?" was all my mother said to that. But the next time Mr. McChesney called her, she was too busy to see him, and the next time after that she was too busy even to talk. She was gluing swatches of fabric to drawings of high fashion clothes printed on cards that announced the opening of Glad Rags. Hundreds of those cards. Allison and I helped.

Even I had advice for her. She was typing address labels, using a phone book and a map of our town with all the fairly well-to-do areas blocked off in red. I said I thought it would save a lot of money on postage if Allison and I and whoever else we could get would ride through those red areas and stick the cards in the mailboxes. That would save postage, and we'd only deliver to houses in expensive sections. The "whoever" I had in mind was Laura. "It pays," I told her when I saw her later. "Not much, but maybe enough to keep you in Twinkies for the rest of the summer."

Just in the nick of time, because Laura was broke for once and facing starvation. Lois was away so much that she didn't bother to stock her freezer, and after six weeks all the crabmeat quiches and miniature Beef Wellingtons had been eaten. Fred was not much help to Laura's situation, because he was on one crash diet after another. Laura's father is a very healthy-looking hypochondriac who was always treating himself for some new and weird ailment that he had recently read about. He went on a protein diet, and then on a carbohydrate diet, and then on a purge of raw carrots, and then he read somewhere that sour cherries would cure arthritis and baldness and raw sauerkraut was a good way to prevent ulcers. Sometimes he fasted. For a while he ate nothing but grapefruit. Laura called him a "faddict." He was also weak-willed, and when Laura was around she was expected not to tempt him away from his diet with anything normal or appetizing. Actually it might have done her some good, but of course I didn't say that. She needed to knock off at least twenty pounds, but that was one subject we couldn't discuss.

Since my mother didn't actually leave her job at Hoffman Engineering until the end of July, all the work at Glad Rags had to be done in her spare time: nights and weekends. She spent lunch hours with bankers, finishing complicated arrangements for financing, and with salesmen, placing orders for stuff she didn't yet have the money to pay for. After all the old stuff had been moved out of Stine's and stored in our garage until my mother could figure out what to do with it, the place had to be cleaned and painted. It took two coats of white paint to cover the mole-colored walls. An electrician put up new light fixtures. A man lettered GLAD RAGS in black and gold across the front window. Salesmen came and went, and the pattern drawers were filled and the notions racks stocked with zippers and seam binding in dozens of colors. Bolts of fabric were stacked all over the place, still wrapped in brown paper.

There was a lot of minor bickering between Mrs. Panek and my mother from the very beginning, but their first major blow-up was about what should go in the small show window. Mrs. Panek favored an up-to-date version of Mr. Stine's pleated fabric, with pattern envelopes pinned on each sample to show how it could be used. My mother said no, you ought to have some things actually made up, because most people have trouble visualizing how a pattern is going to look. Draping it around a mannequin, the way they did it in the broad, brightly lit show windows out at Fabric Town, wasn't enough. Mrs. Panek finally shrugged and said, "Have it your way," and my mother stayed up most of the night sewing a lacy red dress, which she put on her dressmaker's dummy, decorated with a necklace of crystal beads that my father had given her. Then she arranged a little heap of the fabric, leftovers from the cutting, with the things you'd need if you were making it yourself, including the pattern with a photograph of the dress on a model and a little label that said Design Original. Mrs. Panek had to agree that it looked classy, all right. Maybe too classy. Maybe they were going to class themselves right out of business.

I was supposed to help out as a sales clerk, and I was scared to death. I have never been able to sell anything, not even Girl Scout cookies or boxes of candy for our sixth grade trip to Washington, D.C., or Christmas cards. My father was the only person who ever bought anything from me.

"Relax," my mother said. "All the prices are marked on the end of the bolt. Cottons are there, synthetics there, wool over there, silks behind them, linens here, and a group of unusual things—the imports and so on, will be on this front table." She went on showing me things. "Eventually we'll get signs up, so everybody will be able to find the knits and whatever. Meanwhile, all you really have to do is be pleasant. Most people like to look around, but some want you practically to tell them what to buy. If you don't know something, ask me. Or Gloria—if she's still working here," she added.

What I wanted to ask was, "What am I doing here? Where am I going?" Things like that. Not the right questions under the circumstances.

The store was not due to open until ten o'clock, but we were there before eight, frantically trying to do the things we had been too tired to do the night before. Not all of the merchandise had come in. The pigeons had been busy out front, and the sidewalk had to be scrubbed. The red-and-white striped awning with Glad Rags lettered on it that was ordered to replace the green one, frayed and ragged that fluttered "Stine's Fabrics" in faded gray letters, still had not arrived, in spite of many phone calls. At a quarter of ten a truck from Pete's Shade and Awning pulled up in front of the store and began setting up ladders and a metal scaffolding. My mother was furious, but she didn't send him away. Pete and his helper had the old awning draped across the doorway, so no one could go in or out, as the church clock struck ten.

"We're in business," my mother said with a brave smile.

"Where are the customers?" Allison demanded. My mother had made her a tartan plaid back-to-school dress just like the one in the pattern book for September. She looked like a tubby Skotch Kooler, and she kept yanking up the white knee socks that my mother had talked her into wearing to complete the picture.

"They'll be here," Mom said, sounding confident.

At ten thirty Mr. McChesney arrived with a photographer from the *Sentinel* and a large plant with purple foil around the pot and a big red ribbon with GOOD LUCK GLAD RAGS stuck on it in fancy gold paper letters. He shook Mom's hand and kissed her on the cheek. "It's going to be a fabulous success," he said. "How's the crowd?"

"Our clientele doesn't get up this early."

"Maybe you didn't advertise enough."

"They'll start pouring in around noon."

Mr. McChesney glanced meaningfully at the sky. It was clouding up. "It may just be *pouring*."

"A good omen," my mother said stubbornly.

The mayor of our town strolled in then, a flabby man in a limp shirt with crossed tennis rackets embroidered on the pocket.

"Good morning, Mr. Mayor," Mr. McChesney said heartily, grabbing the mayor's hand. "Good of you to come by. This is Mrs. Poindexter, proprietress of Greenfield's newest, chic-est, most prestigious, and potentially most prosperous boutique."

I could see my mother cringing as she accepted the mayor's outstretched hand. "How do you do, Mayor Farwell."

Allison stared at him bug-eyed. "How come he isn't wearing a uniform?" she whispered to me.

"Hello, hello, hello, good people," the mayor said, as though he were launching into a campaign speech.

"Let's get going," said the photographer. "There's a pet show over in the park and I gotta get out there next."

"What are you going to take a picture of?" my mother asked.

"Rabbits, turtles, whatever."

"She means here," Mr. McChesney explained. "A ribbon-cutting ceremony, perhaps?"

Mrs. Panek began to string some seam binding across the front door for a ribbon, but the photographer said it was so narrow it wouldn't show up in the picture. Then I got the idea of cutting a long strip of fabric to use instead. The awning men moved their ladders. The mayor stepped forward and pretended to cut the fake ribbon with our big scissors while my mother and Allison and I and Mrs. Panek "looked on," as it said in the caption, Mrs. Panek holding the potted plant that Mr. McChesney had brought. The photographer took three different shots and then wrote

185

down our names on a card he carried in his pocket. He left for the pet show and the mayor shook hands with us and padded away in his tennis shoes saying, "Good luck, good luck."

Mr. McChesney hung around inspecting everything in the shop and feeling some of the cloth on the bolts. My mother paid no attention to him, which was rather difficult because there were no customers to pay any attention to.

The morning passed slowly. The awning people left. Mr. McChesney left. My mother drank coffee. Allison sighed deeply several times, until Mom sent her out for ice cream. At noon we ate the lunch we had brought from home, using the desk in the back office as a table. We moved the sample book and swatches and papers onto the floor and Allison made another trip to the ice cream store to bring us something cold to drink. The idea had been that we would take turns between customers to sneak back to the office for a bite to eat, but since there was nobody coming in we sat around glumly, eating food we weren't even hungry for. Just when we all had our mouths full of ham and cheese on rye, a little bell tinkled to announce that someone had come in. We all jumped up and rushed out.

It was Laura. "Geez," she said. "Looks nice. Where is everybody?"

"That's what we'd like to know."

I offered her half of my sandwich.

A few minutes later her father appeared and gazed around at the results of his advice. My mother had taken only part of it.

"I thought we had decided on orange accents," Fred Montgomery said.

"You decided that. I hate orange. I used red instead."

"Red is trite."

"Red trite and blue," Laura offered.

"Laura, that's awful," we all said.

My mother offered Fred something to eat, but it was his week for a raw carrot purge. Laura finished the sandwich half and left with her father.

Our first real customer was a woman who came in with her little boy to look at some material for covering pillows. My mother showed her the batik prints from Indonesia and the Finnish silk screens, but she ended up buying a yard and a half of black and white checked gingham from Mr. Stine's old stock. While she was paying, her little boy yanked one of the wire holders off the end of a table, and half-dozen bolts of fabric slumped to the floor.

"Not our kind," Mrs. Panek said after they left with the little piece of gingham in one of our snappy red bags.

Then a yellow sports car slid into the parking place in front of the store, and a well-dressed woman got out, put a dime in the meter, and stared for a long time at our window display. "This one is," my mother said. We all held our breaths and pretended not to watch her.

Finally the woman came in. She wore huge sunglasses, which she did not take off. "Do you have that in a size eight?" she asked, pointing at the red dress in the window.

My mother explained that we didn't sell dresses but that she could make it herself.

"I see," she said. "Thank you." And left.

No one said a word. Then my mother said, "I shouldn't have let her get away. I should have offered to make it for her."

"You're crazy," Mrs. Panek said.

Two girls in jeans came in and asked us to put a poster in the window advertising a high school music club concert.

Two older ladies with gray hair set like icing on a cake were next. They examined everything very carefully. "We're just looking," they explained, but when they left we heard one say to the other, "Fabric Town is cheaper."

"You get what you pay for," Mrs. Panek muttered in the same tone so that the icing-haired ladies might be able to hear her, too.

The afternoon dragged by. "It's probably the heat," I said to my mother, whose bright smile was getting dimmer by the minute. "Everybody's probably at the beach."

"Which is probably where we should be, too. And come back to open after Labor Day."

The thunderstorm that had been collecting all day burst over town like a water-filled balloon. It was much cooler after it passed—cool enough to open the door without letting all the air-conditioning leak out.

A young woman pushed a drooling baby in a stroller through the open door and hauled a length of material and a pattern out of her shopping bag. She bought a zipper, thread, and seam binding to match it. "They were all out of this shade at Fabric Town," she explained. While she made her choices, her baby made passes at the dangling ends of cloth with its slimy hands.

Another forty-five minutes went by.

"We might as well close up early and go home," Mom said. "No way to spend a summer vacation, is it?"

"I don't mind," I lied, because it was just such a lousy Grand Opening.

188

My mother rang up "no sale" and the cash register drawer shot open. She checked the receipts: five dollars and thirty-seven cents, not including sales tax. She chunked the drawer shut again. But then we all spotted another car, a big blue one, shuttling awkwardly back and forth into the parking space in front of the shop, like a crab trying to get into a hole too small for it. I recognized Moozy at the wheel. Finally, thanks to power steering and patience, she managed to lodge her blue yacht fairly close to the curb. I didn't think Moozy looked like a woman who could thread her own needle; she's not the kind of person I would have picked as our customer. But she marched in as though she was planning to rent the place.

"I came by," she said, her false eyelashes pulling everything in like rakes, "to wish the best of luck to Greenfield's new shop." She suddenly noticed me. "Well, I do declare" —she had declared her Southern origins again—"I seem to run into you everywhere I go, Miz C.C. Poindexter."

"This is my mother," I said. "It's her shop." Then I introduced the baroness to my mother as the real estate agent who was Aunt Charlotte's friend. They said "How do you do?" and "I am so thrilled to make youah acquaintance after all this *taaahm*." Meanwhile Moozy's eyes were swinging up and down the display tables.

"What gorgeous things y'all have here, Miz Poindexter! I just love textiles! All those wonderful colors . . . I just love blue, and there are so many shades to choose from. And the textures! I just adore them. I want to *drink in* those colors, *bathe* myself in the feel of them!"

"Do you sew, Mrs. von Schmidt?" my mother asked.

"No, I'm sorry to say I have never mastered the art of the needle, but I would dearly love to know how—"

"We can teach you. We'll be starting classes in the fall."

"We will?" Mrs. Panek asked, sounding surprised. My mother shot her a "shut up, please" look.

"How perfectly lovely! If I only had taaahm . . ."

"Meanwhile we have a seamstress who can sew your dress or whatever you want, to order."

This time I was surprised, but I kept my mouth shut, remembering the woman who had wanted the dress in the window.

"Marvelous! I think while I'm here, then, maybe I ought to order a few things." She began fingering among the blues.

The baroness was there for nearly an hour, past closing time, picking three complicated Vogue patterns, a suit and two dresses, one long with a tear-drop neckline and pleats. Then the fabric and notions. "I'll just take your measurements," my mother said, reaching for a tape measure, "and pass them on to our seamstress."

"Oh, my dear, she doesn't happen to be French, does she? I lived in Paris for a while, you see, when I was married to my first husband, and I have never been so well dressed as when Suzette was doing my things."

"Not French, no. Italian," Mom said. "They're even more reliable."

They settled on a price that sounded astronomical to me, but Moozy didn't even blink an inch-long eyelash. My mother bundled the material and patterns and put them on her desk, moving aside the leftovers from our lunch.

Moozy fluttered her fingers as she left. "I'm going to send all my friends here," she called over her shoulder.

The car parked ahead of hers had gone, and she sailed away from the curb like a ship from its pier.

As soon as we got home that evening, Mom cleared off the dining room table and spread out the first length of blue wool. She worked all evening until after midnight and every night that week and all day Sunday. "Call me Rumplestiltskin," she said above the hum of the sewing machine. At the end of two weeks the three outfits were finished, my mother had dark circles under her eyes, and there were a few customers coming into the store, most of them sent by Moozy.

"What's the dressmaker's name?" one of them asked.

"Margaretta," my mother answered—the Italian version of her own name.

It was Margaretta, Mom said later, who made the difference between survival and disaster through those first weeks. The little Italian seamstress kept our noses above water, but my mother, nearly exhausted, looked as though she might go under at any time.

Chapter Eleven

 It was Laura's idea to have a birthday party. "We'll invite tons of people."

"I don't know tons of people," I said. Neither did she, even though she seemed to know a lot *about* just above everybody. Mostly Laura and I just had each other, which was fine with us but bothered my mother. Mom said I should have more than one friend, more than just Laura. She said it was a mistake to depend on one person, because if something happened, if you had a fight or something, there was no one to fall back on. Also, you needed to be exposed to the ideas of more than just one person.

All of this probably made a lot of sense, and I couldn't really argue with her, but I just didn't know what to do about it. I got along fine with people at school, but after three o'clock they didn't think about me much, I guess, and I didn't think about them much or about the parties I didn't get invited to or the camping trips nobody ever mentioned to me. Actually that's only half true; the first half.

My mother said I should give some parties myself, that if I didn't get invited anywhere it was my own fault for not inviting people to my house. That idea would start her off remembering when *she* was fifteen or sixteen and in high school, which is one of those things about adults, especially parents; they always remember what it was like to be young, or they think they remember, but I don't trust their memories. And I didn't really want to invite those kids from school, because I don't much like parties no matter who is giving them.

But this birthday party turned out to be different. Karen Miller and Sam Lewis were the only other invited guests. Allison was not an invited guest, but she came anyway. Sam, besides being black, is an acolyte in the Episcopal Church. Karen's parents are Jewish liberals, but they are not *that* liberal, and they have made Karen stop seeing Sam at least four times in the past two years. But Karen's parents could see that breaking them up doesn't work, so they were planning to send her far away to a college where she would meet "her own kind"—I guess other people with their liberal viewpoint. Sam was trying to get a scholarship, but his grades aren't terrific and he's not much of an athlete. He's just a nice guy.

I had told my mother that Allison and I were both spending the night with Laura to celebrate my birthday. I neglected to say where, hoping she'd just assume we would be at Lois's farmhouse. This was another thing that had changed completely since my mother got involved with Glad Rags. She now no longer had to know where we were every minute of the time. It wasn't that she didn't care; she just had a lot of things on her mind. It took us a while to catch on to this, but once we did it was great. She even stopped being nervous about us riding our bikes.

Laura got Allison to look around in our attic and find our Christmas tree lights, and the two of them had swagged the strings of red, blue, green, and gold bulbs across the front of Charlotte's house, around a huge sign made out of shelf paper that said HAPPY BIRTHDAY C.C. They moved an old table out of the shed and covered it with more white shelf paper with a big sixteen painted on a piece taped to hang down in front. Paper plates and napkins had been decorated with the date and a lion face, which Allison explained was my astrological sign, in case I didn't know already. Each napkin had a fortune written on it with predictions of good luck for everybody, especially me.

When Allison and I bumped down the rough gravel driveway on our bikes, Sam started playing "Happy Birthday to You" on his harmonica while Laura grinned and Karen snapped my picture. The first picture was of me and the rest were of Sam. The camera, a Nikon with a zoom lens, was a present when her parents split up, to give her an interest so she would not be too broken up by their break-up, to keep her mind off things. Then they gave her a darkroom when they got back together again and began going off on little second and third honeymoons without her. She and Sam spent a lot of time in the darkroom, which her father the doctor had had built in the basement.

There were presents stacked around on the table with the food, and I got busy opening them. Laura had given me a big black ledger book and a small steel file box with blank three by five cards so I could set up a system for keeping track of whatever I felt I needed a system for keeping track of. Allison gave me a box of incense, which she really loves and considers sinful, like black underpants. Karen and Sam gave me a funny hat made out of patches with a floppy brim that drooped over one eye. "Suits you perfectly," Karen said when I put it on, and Sam jazzed a few more bars of "Happy Birthday."

Then we attacked the food. Everybody contributed something. "From each according to his ability," Laura intoned, and Sam added, "To each according to his need" as he loaded a paper plate.

Laura had made a birthday cake but had somehow forgotten the baking powder, and the cake came out of the oven exactly one inch high. She made up for that by smothering it in whipped cream, about two inches of it. The cake was set on a box on the table draped with a napkin, and there were blue candles on it leaning in sixteen different directions. Everything else was arranged around this centerpiece. Allison had brought a jar of peanut butter, snitched from the cupboard at home, and a jar of sweet pickles, a special passion of hers which she told me twice she had bought with her own money. Laura had provided a jar of imported English jam, a can of truffled liver paté, and a loaf of spongey white bread. Karen contributed half a leftover roast beef, crispy brown on the outside, pinker toward the middle, reddish in the center. Karen was one of the kids who always had some delicious lunch from home and gave it away because she preferred the school food. Sam brought a half-gallon of ice cream, which he got at a special rate because he works part time at Super Cool.

While we were still eating, Laura set up her tape deck

195

and put on some music. Karen jumped up and started dancing. "Come on everybody," she said. "Group dancing, just like in camp." She moved gracefully, coaxing us. Sam joined her with supple shoulder movements and elaborate footwork. Then Laura, heavy-footed and not quite with the rhythm, began to swing her hips back and forth. Allison is an amazingly good dancer; for such a tubby little girl she moves easily. I watched from the hammock until Allison tipped it over and I sprawled on the ground. Then I got up and danced, too, something I didn't do often. Somebody *always* used to ask if I wasn't afraid I'd get my hair snagged in the overhead wires.

I don't know which of us was aware first of the two boys standing there watching us. They were little older then us, and they wore cut-off jeans and battered hats. One had a blond beard; the other one wore gold-rimmed eyeglasses. Both carried enormous backpacks and wore heavy hiking boots that called attention to their feet. The blond one had on one green sock and one yellow. The one in glasses wore two blue socks, one longer and darker than the other with a white stripe around the top. I recognized first the trademark of Wisdom Peak and second, behind the blond beard, my cousin Michael.

"Hello, Michael," I hollered above the noise of the music. Then Laura hit the Off button, and it was suddenly quiet.

"Hey, C.C.!" Michael whooped, and he gave me a big hug that I could not return because of his towering backpack. And it was the first time he had ever done anything like that. "What's happening?" he asked. He looked around at the colored lights and the table full of leftover food. He didn't recognize Allison at first.

"We're having a party," I explained. "It's my birthday. Put down your packs and have some food."

Then everybody came to life, as though they were frozen statues suddenly defrosted. We all introduced each other and there was a lot of handshaking. Brian, the guy with glasses, said they were on their way to explain the philosophy of Wisdom Peak to a city commune in New Haven, and then they were going on up to Boston and Maine, speaking to some groups that were interested in what they were doing. A good-will tour, they called it. They were hitchhiking most of the way and camping out.

"So we came here to spend the night, and to get my mother to feed us. By the way," he said, accepting a plate from Allison with a pile of food on it, "where is Charlotte?"

"In Massachusetts at an art colony," I said.

"I'm house-sitting for her," Laura explained. "But you're certainly welcome to stay here."

"Terrific," Brian said. He had taken off his boots and was walking around in his socks, getting more food. They both attacked the provisions as though they hadn't seen anything like it in days.

"His socks don't match," Allison said to me.

"They're not supposed to."

Michael heard us. "How do you know about the socks?"

"My sister knows all about Wisdom Peak," Allison boasted. "She's going to go there to live."

Brian and Michael looked at me with new interest. "No kidding! You are? When?"

"Soon as I can get it worked out," I mumbled. I was dying to talk to them about it, but not there or then.

My answer irritated Allison. "She's going to visit as soon as Aunt Charlotte comes back, with the money she's getting paid for feeding Hugo and taking care of the garden and all. Laura and I are helping her. For nothing," she added, suddenly aware of the injustice.

"Why don't you come too, Allison?" Michael asked her. I didn't remember that my cousin's voice was so deep.

"Why don't *y'all* come?" Brian drawled.

"You mean that, man?" Sam asked. "All of us?" Sam and Karen were snuggled together on the hammock.

"Sure," Michael said. "Why not?"

"I want to hear it from Brian, too."

"Everybody," Brian said. "Everybody's welcome. Only problem might be with Allison. She's too young."

"I am not," Allison said glumly.

"Well, they have these rules, see. If one of your parents came, that would be okay, but C.C. isn't old enough to take responsibility for you."

"I am so," I said, in just the same tone of voice as Allison, and everybody laughed.

"It's a legal thing," Michael said.

"Just for a visit?"

"I thought you meant you were all coming to stay there."

"Some are, some aren't," I said vaguely. I didn't want Allison to know I was planning to go there to live.

But Allison's mind was elsewhere. "You know what we forgot? Sam's ice cream!" Food always took precedence, and she trundled off to the freezer to bring back the last course.

After we had eaten the ice cream with little chunks of my flat birthday cake, Michael got up and disappeared into the house—his mother's house. When he came out again he said, "I'd almost forgotten the luxury. First thing I'm going to do tonight is take a hot bath."

"Just be sure you clean out the tub when you're done," Laura said.

"Yes, *ma'am*."

Allison's eyes were wide open. Allison hates to take baths. "What luxury?"

"Bathroom."

"Don't you have one at Wisdom Peak?"

"Yes. That's just it. *One*. For forty people. We do have a couple of outhouses, though, and an outdoor shower, but its shut off in the winter."

You could see Allison's brain running from one thing to another, seizing something, studying it, running on to something else, just by the expression on her face. A whole winter of not taking a bath—that was fine. But having to take a cold shower in the summer—that was something else. Actually, the only thing she could put up with was a warm bubble bath, for fun, with lots of toys under the suds. But the outhouses: "Like in state parks? Outhouses like those?"

"Not nearly that classy," Michael said. "A wooden board with three holes cut in it. But we *are* pouring concrete floors for them this summer."

"Three holes," Allison echoed.

"Yup. Real toilet paper, though."

Meanwhile Brian was working his way down through another pile of sliced roast beef. He and Michael had just about demolished Karen's roast. He saw me watching him. "Fantastic," he said, with his mouth full. "Haven't had meat like this in I don't know how long. How long would you say it's been, Michael?"

"Weeks," he answered, mouth full. "Months maybe."

"Are you vegetarian?" Allison asked, discouragement spreading across her round face like a rash.

"No, no. Only sometimes it works out that way. Listen, we had possum a couple of weeks ago, and it wasn't half bad."

"Possum?" Allison shrieked.

"Not half bad, but not half good, either," Michael put in.

"It's a common dish around there. Some of the local folks showed us how to clean it and cook it."

"Ugh," we all said.

"Listen, the food there is terrific," Michael said, the evangelist. "You sign up for cooking—I'll explain about the labor credit system in a minute—and everybody who wants that job seems to have a couple of specialties, so you don't get sick of anybody's style. And things like possum stew are really rare. My own specialty is macaroni and cheese with a lot of other stuff thrown in, and everybody really likes it a lot."

"Must be an old family recipe," Laura said, looking at me.

Brian said, "Remember the time I was on for breakfast, and I popped up a whole vat of popcorn and served it with milk and sugar?"

"Yeah. Nobody would eat that, either."

Allison was pulling up handfuls of grass. "I've decided not to go," she said. One convert lost.

But Karen, Sam, and even Laura were listening to every word Michael and Brian said. Those two in their unmatched socks had their audience in the palms of their hands with messages of peace, freedom, fresh air, and the good life—all things that I knew about from reading "Pearls of Wisdom." Brian and Michael knew how to handle an audience. Michael was the fervent one who saw only the good things about Wisdom Peak. Anything that wasn't perfect right now would certainly be that way in the very near future. Brian drawled just the right amount of reality to keep it from sounding like a propaganda exercise. You heard him, but if you had already accepted the idea of community clothes and labor credits and having all your work go for the benefit of the whole group, you weren't really put off by stories of outhouses and peculiar food.

After a while we got back to having a party. Brian played his guitar. Michael whipped out a recorder. And of course Sam had his harmonica. They all took turns playing, and we danced and sang. Michael taught us some of the dances they do at Wisdom Peak. Soon the last bit of melted ice cream had been lapped up, and there wasn't a crumb of birthday cake left. Suddenly I felt very tired. Karen was making motions of cleaning up. "We got to get going," she said.

"Oh, leave it," Laura said through a big yawn. "We'll catch it all in the morning." Which meant, I guessed, I'd get to clean up after my own birthday party.

"Whyn't y'all stay?" Brian asked.

"Hey, yeah," Michael chimed in. "We could all sleep right here in the yard. My brother Jebby and I used to do that all the time. It'll give you an idea of what communal living is all about." He started planning and organizing. "Brian and I have sleeping bags, and two of you can sleep in that hammock easy enough."

"That's us," Sam said. He and Karen had hardly been out of it all evening. Her parents must have been away again.

"C.C., you and Laura and Allison can bring mattresses out here from the living room."

"There are only two mattresses," Allison pointed out.

"Floor pillows," Laura reminded her.

We obediently dragged the corduroy-covered foam slabs out of the living room along with the big, squashy pillows, and put them on the grass. When Michael said we ought to put something under them to protect them from the damp grass, we rooted around in the shed until we found a big tarp. Then Allison, who always is trying to con somebody into getting her a drink during the night, decided it would be a good idea to have a bottle of water next to her in case she woke up. Brian and Michael went off to take hot showers. Allison began complaining that the floor pillows kept sliding apart. When Brian and Michael finished in the bathroom, Laura inspected and reported remarkably little water damage for two males accustomed to primitive conditions.

Finally there were seven human bodies, plus Hugo, strewn around the front yard. We lay and looked up at the stars and I thought it was the best birthday I had ever had and must be a sign of better days ahead. I said so, and everyone agreed I was absolutely right. I went to sleep.

Partly because we were all so tired, and partly because Laura's warning system was rigged to go off in the house, not outside, nobody heard the buzzer or the car pull into the driveway. Except Allison, who was drinking out of her water bottle and heard the crunch on the gravel. Still half-asleep, she ran into the house and plugged in the Christmas tree lights. I don't know why she did that; neither does she. When I woke up seconds later, headlights were glaring in my face. Next to me I could make out Laura on her knees, clutching a sheet around her, shielding her eyes. A man's voice muttered, "What the hell is going on here?" Nobody moved.

Except Hugo, who bounded across the grass faster than he had moved since Allison stole his rubber mouse. Then a second voice, which I thought was my aunt's, was saying, "Hi, boy! Down, Hugo, down!"

The blinding headlights cut off, and into the blackness darted two small shafts of light. It was Mr. McDermott and Charlotte with flashlights. Total confusion followed, with everybody talking at once while everybody tried to explain.

I explained that it was my birthday, and Laura explained that she was helping me take care of the house, and Allison explained that we were having a party. Next Michael introduced Brian and explained about their trip. Charlotte hugged Michael and explained that she and Mr. McDermott had decided to leave the art colony because none of the other artists seemed really serious about their work and spent too much time drinking beer and playing Frisbee. Then Mr. McDermott—Phil—explained that they had both decided not to go back to their teaching jobs in the fall. Instead they were going to drive the purple van all around the country for a year, and he was going to write poetry about their experiences and she was going to do a sketchbook of Americana to go with the poems. Charlotte said they were going to get jobs along the way when they needed money, and that would give them an insight into what other Americans are thinking and doing. Also, she said, she wanted to visit Jebby out in Oregon. Karen and Sam said they were thinking about going to Wisdom Peak with Michael and Brian. The only one without much to say was Laura, who sat shooting daggers at my aunt and casting lovesick glances at Phil McDermott. For a sensible girl, she can be very dumb.

Charlotte and Phil had some food in the van, so we all ate some more and talked about our future plans, most of which we had just worked out in the past couple of hours. I, now sixteen years old, sat quietly and listened. Because all of a sudden I wasn't sure Wisdom Peak was what I wanted. It didn't have anything to do with three-holed outhouses and possum for dinner. It had to do with me.

"Well, C.C.," said my aunt, "seems you've had a busy summer. Tell me all about it."

I was tired and I didn't really want to tell her or anybody else all about it. "Too much happened," I said. "It would take days."

"Good," she said. "Let's start tomorrow. I guess it already *is* tomorrow. I mean later, after we've had some rest." Then she and Phil McDermott pulled their sleeping bags and air mattresses out of the purple van and all nine of us settled down to sleep.

The sun woke us the next morning. Everyone seemed a little embarrassed in the bright light of day. Aunt Charlotte invited us all to stay for breakfast, but Laura reminded her quietly that there really wasn't much to eat. Michael and Brian said they wanted to get an early start and they'd eat later. They slung their packs on their backs and started off for the turnpike to hitch a ride to New Haven. Mr. McDermott offered to give them a lift on his way to his old apartment. As the van labored out of the driveway, I noticed that somebody had painted out the WOMAN POWER sign above the rear engine and replaced it with a new one: READ A POEM EVERY DAY.

Karen and Sam left hand in hand. Allison rode her bike home to tell Mom I'd be in the store in a little while. That left Laura and me with Charlotte. We told my aunt the whole story of Laura's move for independence. It was the kind of tale she loved. "Listen," she said, "I want to try again to rent the house, this time on a long-term lease, while Phil and I are gone." I don't think she saw Laura wince. "So why don't you stay here until and if I get a tenant. You obviously did a great job."

It really did look a lot neater than it had when Charlotte left in June. The teapot was out again, and one of Charlotte's smoky herb teas was brewing in it. We sat on the floor around the low table. Laura had waxed and polished the tree-slice to a satin glow, and when Charlotte started to set the teapot down on it, Laura dashed to the kitchen for a hot mat to put under it.

"What are you going to do about Hugo?" Laura asked, crossing her legs and lowering herself heavily onto a floor cushion. She still didn't quite have the knack. "He's what makes it hard to rent."

"I know that, I know." Charlotte sighed. "And I don't have the answer. We thought of taking him along, but he's so big." We all thought for a while. "I don't really want to have to give him away."

Hugo knew he was being discussed. He moved closer to us and sprawled again on the floor, keeping one sleepy eye on us.

"I'll take him," Laura said. "My mother has a little

205

farm now, and a goat. She'll hardly notice Hugo. She's never home anyway, and I know she'll love him."

"You'd better ask first, just to be sure she'd love him if she does happen to notice him." Hugo was beginning to snore.

Finally Laura said she ought to go, and I got up to go, too, promising to come back soon. My mother was expecting me to help her out at Glad Rags, and I pedaled home, showered, changed, actually hung up my jeans and put my underwear in the hamper, and rode down to the store.

Everything was in an uproar. Mrs. Panek was threatening to quit again. My mother tried to calm her down, but with a toss of her head which knocked her new blond wig slightly askew she marched out of the store just as some customers strolled in. My mother motioned me to deal with a worried-looking woman with stringy brown hair snatched back in a ponytail and a faded sundress that was too big around the bust. She might have been pretty, but she looked as though she hadn't slept for days and had maybe been crying a lot or had hay fever. Her eyes were puffy.

"May I help you?"

She answered through a wet Kleenex. "I'm looking for something"—sniffle sniffle—"to make me look beautiful."

I cleared my throat. "Do you want to look beautiful sexy or beautiful sweet?" I asked her.

"Both."

My mother was busy with two sets of serious customers, and I couldn't ask her for help. I was nervous, but this woman looked so miserable that her misery drowned out my nervousness. I wanted to help her feel better. And so I, who never had much sense at all about what goes with what for myself, looked at her weepy blue eyes and somehow knew exactly what would be right for her. I showed her one thing and then another and let her hold the fabric up around her face and look at herself in a narrow mirror stuck on a pillar in the middle of the store. After a few minutes she began to brighten up, and we took out three bolts of fabric that she liked and laid them on the counter while she looked through the pattern books. She said she didn't really know how to sew very well, and since that put us pretty much in the same category I helped her find something I figured I could handle without getting too tied up. It didn't take her long to decide, and I wrote up the sale including all the zippers and snaps, without any problems. When my customer left, she was looking better than when she came in, as though I had found the secret formula and it was already starting to work.

My mother was beaming at me. "Good job, C.C.," she said. I felt fine.

There are turning points in everyone's life, just as Baroness Moozy von Schmidt said when she wanted me to clarify my values at the rap session all those months ago. It doesn't have to be a historic moment, like Newton getting hit on the head with an apple. It can be a much quieter thing, maybe so quiet you don't even notice it too much at the time, but it makes a tremendous difference in everything that happens after that. The sale I made that day was a turning point for me.

Not that I immediately organized my closet, or my life, or became the most popular girl in my class. But I found out that I really liked working in the store and that I was good at it. For the rest of August I went there every day. When school started, I worked after school and Thursday night and all day Saturday. My mother didn't try to replace Mrs. Panek. I was it.

I was therefore much too busy to take the trip to Wisdom Peak, and I didn't have time to regret it. Laura went instead, with Michael and Brian and Hugo. She loved it, and she's planning to go there to live. She is working on her parents to give their permission. She threw away all of her ledgers and her careful plans.

My father and his new wife bought a farm in the country, and we go out to visit them sometimes. Libby still organizes everything. Jennifer and Allison still have huge battles that end with much kissing and making up. My father is doing okay. We're pretty good friends. My mother and I get along very well in the store, where she treats me like an adult, and not so well at home, where she doesn't. Alex McChesney doesn't come around any more. Every now and then she meets a new man and goes into an uproar about that for a while. "It's okay not to be in love," she says, but I don't think she means it. I'd like to have somebody love my mother.

One day a guy came in and asked me to put up a poster in our show window for a series of art classes. I showed him where to tack it—we have a big bulletin board for all these announcements, and then we show a pattern for dresses that you could make to wear to the events that are advertised. An embroidered smock for the art classes, and so on. That was my idea. Then I signed up for the classes myself. We do charcoal sketching; I'm better than I thought I would be. The guy's name is Ed and he's two inches shorter than I am and very funny. I guess you could say we're getting to be friends.

Other news: I grew another half inch. Six feet two. Not a Guinness World Record, but tall enough.

It's not bad.